"*I'm not th<u>at b</u>ad...*"

Karen Wyman took out a compact and ran a lipstick over her mouth. She smiled.

"What did you want to see me about, Miss Wyman?" asked Paris.

"Do you get to Eastern City often?"

"Fairly often."

"That's nice," she said. "Maybe we'll see each other again."

"Maybe," Paris said. "What is it you want, Miss Wyman?"

"It's about myself. You must have a horrible opinion of me." She smiled archly. "I'm not *that* bad, really."

But all Wade knew was that a killer was loose. And it might be <u>her</u>!

"A pale horse: and his name
that sat on him was Death."

REVELATION VI, 8

BEWARE
THE
Pale Horse

BY BEN BENSON

WILDSIDE PRESS

Beware the Pale Horse

Published by Wildside Press LLC
wildsidepress.com | bcmystery.com

Beware the Pale Horse

1

FIRST THERE WAS A HILL, AND WADE PARIS, COMING OVER the crest of it, stopped the State Police car and sniffed the salt tang of the air. Below him, the road fell away sharply and dipped to where the Atlantic shimmered blue in the July morning sun. To his left lay White Sands Beach, a half-mile stretch of crescent, cream-colored sand. Slightly to the right of him, Sunset Point jutted out into the sea, dotted sparsely with stunted scrub pines, the lone white two-and-a-half-story house on the very end, standing like a beacon.

Paris took a last drag from his cigarette, crushed it into the dashboard ashtray, and started the car. He drove down the hill, passing the small cove of Sunset Harbor and the half-dozen cabin cruisers anchored behind the tiny breakwater. He entered Sunset Point Road and drove along the barren bluff. A mile down the road he came upon an assortment of cars, with people gathered around them, their heads turned in the direction of the big white house, now turning again to watch his car. Directly ahead of him was the sign reading CHARLES ENDI-COTT—PRIVATE ROAD. Behind it, two massive square stone posts flanked the macadam, and alongside stood a pale-blue State Police sedan. A heavy chain hung between the posts and standing there, straddle-legged, was a State Police trooper.

Paris stopped the car. The trooper came up, looked in and saluted. He went back, unfastened the chain, and let it slack to the ground. Paris drove over it. The road hairpinned around the bluff, rising slightly. He came to a five-foot hedge and behind it was the Endicott house.

The house was huge, with white shingles and black shutters. The roof was flat in the center and on it Paris could see the white railed enclosure of the widow's walk. On either side of the house were concrete paths with small arbors, trellises with roses, clumps of carefully tended flowers, banks of poinsettias, camellias, jasmine. The air was heavy with their scent.

The concrete driveway ran up and under an old-fashioned carriage port. Along the side of it were three more State Police cars and two long, sleek, black official sedans. Paris parked behind them.

There was a cluster of uniformed and civilian-clothed men under the shade of the carriage port. Paris recognized the short, obese figure of Ramspak, the local district attorney. Talking with him were Detective-Lieutenant Paul Coyne and an assistant district attorney. Now a State Police corporal left the group, came up and saluted briskly. Paris returned the salute and stepped out into the strong, hard sunlight.

The corporal said, "The Commissioner is inside. He wants to see you right away, Inspector." Then he hesitated and looked in the direction of the group. "Lieutenant Coyne's been asking for you. Here he comes now."

Coyne came over, a big, heavy-shouldered man of forty with a large, beefy, closely shaven face, large owl-like eyes, and a prematurely balding head. He was wearing expensive white and brown sport shoes, a fawn-colored gabardine suit, a white shirt and a blue silk tie. He shook a limp, hurried hand with Paris. He said, "The Commish is tearing a gut inside, Inspector. He's been waiting for you to show up."

Paris waited for the corporal to go away. "I got here as soon as I could," he said.

"That's okay," Coyne said. He ran his tongue over his full, sensual lips. "You don't have to apologize to me, Wade. It's just that the Commish is new on the job and it makes him kind of anxious. This is a big case. One of the biggest the state ever had. An Endicott has been murdered."

"I know," Paris said. "Charles Endicott's been killed. The Endicotts are important people. But it wasn't only Charles Endicott. Dan Hallmark was killed here last night too. He was a State Police lieutenant. Maybe you've forgotten that, Coyne."

"Now don't get me wrong," Coyne said suavely. He put two

fingers together. "Dan and I were like this. It hit me hard to hear he was knocked off last night. I was telling the newspaper boys how close Dan and I were."

"Don't kid me," Paris said. "You were never close to him—in any respect. But you were always one guy who had time for press conferences. I'd like to see some work too."

Paris turned away and walked toward the house. Coyne watched him, looked down at the concrete driveway and the soft bubbles of tar in the seams. He spat deliberately.

The door to the house opened and a man came out, mopping his face with a large white handkerchief. He looked up, saw Paris, and came over to him. Paris saluted. The Commissioner ignored the salute. He said, "So you finally got here, Paris. Where the hell have you been anyway? It's almost ten o'clock."

"I've been working upstate," Paris said. "I got here as soon as I could."

"I told you to drop everything and hop to it."

"I came as fast as I could," Paris said steadily. "It's a long drive."

"Come on," the Commissioner said abruptly. "We're going for a walk."

They cut across the grass. There was a path leading along the bluff. The Commissioner moved along, large, bulky, an inner tube of fat around his middle, wearing a pencil-striped suit that flapped in the warm sea breeze. There was a big, light-colored hat set slanting on his head, the brim wide and the ribbon narrow. His legs waddled as he walked.

There were a pair of press photographers adjusting a camera tripod on the slight rise of a hill. The Commissioner stopped and watched them. "They're all around us," he said approvingly. "The joint's crawling with them. They've got the AP and UP men here."

Paris said nothing, looking away at the combers as they frothed white against the shore. Close in along the bluff, a star-class sailboat with a blue hull, its jib rippling in the wind, moved in toward the boat basin. At the tiller, a tow-haired boy in a short-sleeved white jersey shortened the sail.

"This case is important to me, Paris," the Commissioner said. "You've got no idea what this thing can lead to if it's handled right. I want to make a big showing. If I do, I'll take care of everybody along the line. That's the kind of guy I am."

Paris didn't answer. The Commissioner took out a cigar, stripped off the cellophane and lit it. He puffed impatiently. "I've got Paul Coyne here to work on it," he said. "Now I know you outrank him, but I want you to sort of let him handle it. If you know what I mean."

"No," Paris said. "What *do* you mean?"

"I don't have anything against you personally, Paris. And Coyne can take his orders from you, in a round-about way, if he has to. But I've got you down in an advisory capacity. So Paul can run the show and that will take care of this rank business. The reason is that I'd like to see Coyne come up and get experience."

"No," Paris said. "What's the real reason, Commissioner?"

The Commissioner studied the end of his cigar very carefully. "Well," he said, "I don't have to beat around the bush with you, Paris. Paul Coyne's a good smart boy but he hasn't worked much on homicides. He knows political angles and he's good with publicity. His brother is Lieutenant-Governor and that doesn't do any harm either, if you know what I mean. You've got to keep things in the family if you want to get along in this world. It'll be a break for Paul if he cracks this thing quick. Certain people are going to appreciate all the help he gets. And if you do us a favor, we'll do a favor back. That's the way things go. But there'll be plenty for everybody. I take care of my friends. That's one thing about me."

Paris, his mouth tightly compressed, didn't answer. He looked away at the ocean. A cabin cruiser creamed the water near the Point, its long deep-sea fishing rods slanting to the sky.

"Of course," the Commissioner said very casually, "if you don't like the set-up, you don't have to go in. It makes no difference with me. I can reassign you."

"No," Paris said tonelessly. "I want to go in. I knew Dan Hallmark since I came into the Department. I know his wife and three kids. Dan was in grade a long time as a lieutenant and I might have passed him. But he still knew a lot and he taught me all he knew. He was a good, conscientious cop and he always did his job. Seventeen years with the Department. He had three years to go for his pension. It was a hell of a way to finish up."

"Sure, sure," the Commissioner said. "I had a press conference this morning. I told the boys how he was a credit to his shield and that we wouldn't stop until we avenged him. In fact, Paul set up press relations in the Town Hall. He had to, with all these newspaper men around. Only they don't have enough telephones." He rubbed his hands briskly. "Now I'll tell you what we want you to do, Paris. I've given Paul all the help he needs. He'll work out from here, the scene of the crime. You'll work on the outside, around the fringes. Now you've been operating from the attorney-general's office and you always reported directly to him, or to your supervisor, Colonel Davies. From now on that's out. You report everything directly to me. I'll funnel it into Paul, and Paul will give the press what he thinks they should have. You were never one to talk to the newspapers anyway. We'll see you get the proper credit when the time comes."

Paris, watching the boat basin, saw the sailboat had moved inside the breakwater. Now it came about into the wind. The boy cast his anchor expertly, the mainsail sliding down and billowing over the hull.

"I'm not looking for credit," Paris said. "There's been a double homicide here, and that's the job. Part of it affects me personally. It's not a Roman holiday and it's not a circus."

"Who said anything about a circus?" the Commissioner said. "What are you trying to do, Paris?"

"I'm just telling you how I feel. I don't like to see you make a circus out of this."

"You're telling *me* what to do, Paris?"

"I'm telling you the way I feel."

"Well, don't tell me. Just mind your business. And I don't

give a damn how big your reputation is, I can cite you for insubordination."

"All right," Paris said. "You do that."

"If I do, I'll suspend you," the Commissioner snapped.

"You can do that too," Paris said.

The Commissioner took the cigar from his mouth. He took out his handkerchief and wiped his forehead. "Now there's no use getting excited," he said genially. "I'm excusing you because you're all upset about Dan Hallmark. I don't want any friction now. Paul can use all the help he can get on this. So I'm going to forget what you said for the sake of the Department." He slapped Paris on the back. "Come on, let's go back and talk to Paul."

They turned back to the house. Coyne was waiting for them at the edge of the driveway, a tight little smile on his face.

"All right, Paul," the Commissioner said. "I've given Paris the set-up and everything is fine. Now you two get together. I'm going over to sweeten up Ramspak. He's complaining we're squeezing him out."

He walked across the driveway to the carriage port. Paris looked along the far end of the bluff. There were a half-dozen troopers in a skirmish line across the underbrush.

"What are they doing?" he asked Coyne.

"Looking for the gun, Wade. I'm combing the whole place."

Paris nodded his head. "You have your report on everything since last night?"

"Sure thing. Why? You want to see it?"

"Yes."

"I'll get it for you," Coyne said. He went away. Paris stood alone in the sun. He took out a cigarette and lit it. His mouth was dry and parched. He dropped the cigarette to the driveway. Coyne came back with a clipboard and handed it to Paris. Paris read it.

"There's nothing here about the local chief of police," Paris said. "Wasn't he in on it?"

"A little," Coyne said. He opened his mouth and yawned. "The chief's only a yokel. I don't need him."

"You're making a mistake. He's important."

"I can handle it without him, Wade. I don't need him."

"Well, *I* need,him. Where is he?"

"I don't know. He's around here somewhere."

"All right," Paris said. "I'll find him. I'll take along a carbon of the report. I'm going in to see Mrs. Endicott."

"We've already spoken to her," Coyne said. "I don't think you need to see her. It's all down on the report. She's got her lawyer, Mr. Hanft, in there. They're making arrangements for her son's funeral."

"I'll talk to her anyway," Paris said.

"What are you so sore about, Wade?"

"I'm not sore," Paris said. "I always knew you were a man with a small mind. I feel a little sorry for you."

2

PARIS WENT ALONG THE CONCRETE PATH THAT SKIRTED the seaward side of the house. He went under a rose arbor. A bird chirped nearby. A man wearing a navy-blue police uniform was coming down the walk toward him. There was a large holstered revolver strapped to his side. Paris, coming up to him, saw the gold-plated shield, the visored cap with the gold band, and the gold-braided insignia with the word *Chief* on it. The man was short, bandy-legged and paunchy. His face was incongruously lean—tanned, leathery, and deeply seamed. There was a small white scar near the corner of his mouth. Paris put out his hand.

"I'm Wade Paris," he said. "You must be the chief of police."

The man took his hand. "I'm Gus Kay," he said. "I'm sure glad to see you, Inspector. They said you were coming."

"We're going to need your help," Paris said.

"Well, that's fine," Kay said. "I've been waiting for something to do. But they've been so busy talking to the newspaper people, they ain't had time for nothing else. It's the first homicide we've ever had at White Sands Beach, so I don't rightly know what the procedure is. But the way they're carrying on, it's kind of sacrilegious. Is that the way the state cops operate all the time?"

"No," Paris said. "Only since we've had a new commissioner."

"Then I'm glad of that," Kay said. "The way they act is mighty queer, Inspector. I've been following your cases, and I keep a file of them, but from what I see, you ain't going to be in charge here."

"No," Paris said.

"That's what I thought. That Coyne and the Commissioner, they're cosy, them two. Everybody can see what's going on. If Coyne solves this case he's going to get himself covered with glory." Kay hesitated. "Maybe I'm talking out of turn but I'll say it anyway. I kind of heard them talking this morning. They've got you here to run interference for Coyne. But if he don't come up with anything, they're going to let you take the rap for it. Did you know that, Inspector?"

Paris nodded his head. "Yes," he said.

"Then it ain't no surprise to you. You're not going to do anything about it?"

"No," Paris said. "You see, I was a friend of Dan Hallmark's."

"Then that makes a difference," Kay said. "I met Dan Hallmark a couple of times. He was a good cop, Inspector."

"Yes," Paris said. "And a good friend. That's why I'd appreciate it if you'd give me a briefing, Chief. I'd like to know about these Endicotts."

"Sure," Kay said. "Maybe we'd better get under those roses where there's some shade. That sun is plenty strong." He went in under the arbor. Paris followed him. Kay reached into his breast pocket and took out a pack of tiny black cigars. He offered one to Paris. Paris shook his head. The Chief lit up. He took off his cap, rubbed his sparse gray hair.

"Well," he said, "the one who was killed was Charles Endicott, Junior. Mr. Charles we always called him. Everybody called him Mr. Charles, even when he was a little shaver. That's because his father died when he was very young. The Endicotts owned almost all of White Sands Beach then, as well as the Point. Gave the beach away to the town, they did. They built the jetties so we'd get some nice sand. They built the wharf and the boat basin and the breakwater. Gave money every year to the Improvement Association. You couldn't ask for finer civic-minded people. Mr. Charles was a handsome young fellow. About your age, Inspector. Tall like you, your shoulders. He was a good boy. Never showed his money." He stopped and shook his head. "Too bad he had to go and get killed like that. But that's what the Endicotts were like."

"Was Mr. Endicott married?" Paris asked.

"No. He was engaged. The girl's name is Karen Wyman. She's been staying at the house here."

"Who else was at the house last night?"

"Mrs. Endicott. She's Mr. Charles's mother. Then they've got two people in the servants' wing. Elizabeth and Henry Davis. Elizabeth is the housekeeper and her husband is the handy man. They've also got a cook who comes in days."

"Who else do the Endicotts know here at the beach?"

"The Endicotts never socialized much. Only a few friends. There's George Hanft, their lawyer. He owns a big house on the beach. Then there's an artist named Walter Almieda. He was a friend of Mr. Charles. He has a cottage on the beach too. Then, of course, there's Mr. Noble. He's staying at the White Sands Apartments. He ain't really a friend. He works for the Endicotts."

"What kind of work?" Paris asked.

"He's a curator over at the Eastern City Art Museum. That's where they have the Endicott Collection of Asiatic Art. This Mr. Noble handles it. The Endicotts have a big name in art."

"I know," Paris said. "All right, let's get back to last night. I understand you were the first police official at the scene. Maybe you can tell me what happened."

"Well, I guess I can. But don't you have it in the report?"

"Yes. But I'd like to hear your version too."

"Thanks," Kay said. "I appreciate that. Nobody else yet has wanted me to talk about it. Last night, being Monday night, I was playing cards over at the White Sands Apartments. That's owned by Eddie Hansen and he's the chairman of the board of selectmen. We play poker over there every Monday night. It's only a penny-ante game, but we've been playing there in Apartment Eleven for years now. I was holding a king-high flush and I was just about to give the pot a little bump. Al Coats came busting in to yell that Mr. Charles had been killed."

"Who is Al Coats?"

"He's my special. He's a good kid. I work him nights during the summer season. He rides the car around. Coats told me the operator called him on the car telephone that Mr. Charles and another man were reported dead. He was patrolling the lower end of the beach then. He came and told me. I left the card game."

"What time was it then?"

"Almost five past nine. I didn't sound the siren. I put on the red spot blinker I have on the roof of the car and I took Al Coats with me and got over to the Endicott house. I saw Mr. Charles on the floor of the library and next to him, all huddled up, I recognized Dan Hallmark. They were both dead. I left young Coats guarding the library and I went into the hall and telephoned the Newgate Barracks."

"And you didn't touch anything?"

"I'm only a country cop," Kay said. "I wouldn't go in and putter around. I know better than that."

"Where was Hallmark's gun?"

"That's what I looked to see first. It was in his holster and it hadn't been fired. No, sir, that gun never left his holster."

"Now Coyne has something else down. He says on the way

to the Endicott house you met no cars. But you did see a small boat with an outboard motor. It was coming into the boat basin."

"Yes," Kay said, fingering his belt holster. "To tell the truth, I didn't give it a thought then. I couldn't see who was in the boat and I was anxious to get over to the house. Then Coyne tells me that the killer was in that boat and that I muffed it. I had the killer and I didn't know it." ·

"But you had no way of knowing," Paris said.

"But I had him. That's what gripes me." He shook his head sadly. "I still don't know what Dan Hallmark was doing there."

"I'm going to tell you that," Paris said. "But first, let's get the time straightened out. You say it was about five past nine when Coats came to the White Sands Apartments?"

"Yes."

"You left there and rode over to the Endicott house. You got there about ten past nine?"

"Yes."

"When did Mr. Noble show up?"

"At nine-thirty. He drove up and said he had an appointment with Mr. Charles. He was shocked when I told him Mr. Charles was dead. I sent him upstairs to be with Mrs. Endicott. Five minutes later the troopers came from the Newgate Barracks, and five minutes after that Lieutenant Coyne showed up with the lab men. And at ten o'clock, the D. A. came with his assistants. Then they kept coming so fast I lost track."

"And from then on Lieutenant Coyne took over?"

"That's right. I still don't know what's going on."

"You might as well know," Paris said. "It's your town. According to Coyne's report, Mr. Endicott had a visitor last Friday afternoon. It was a young man, not too well dressed, good-looking, not more than twenty-one years of age, reddish-blond hair, tall, and rather thin. He wouldn't give his name. He said he had something to sell. He had a box with him and he opened it up and inside was the statue of a horse. Endicott thought it was a rare Chinese antique and he was interested. The boy wanted ten thousand dollars for it."

There was a small wrought-iron bench in the rose arbor. Paris sat down. Kay watched him stoically.

"All right," Paris said. "Ten thousand dollars for the statue of a horse. It's a lot of money. But Endicott would pay it if he knew it wasn't stolen from somewhere. He asked the boy where he got it but the boy was evasive. Endicott asked him to leave the statue. That was so his curator, John Noble, could examine it to see if the statue was genuine. The boy refused to do this. However he did agree to bring back the statue Monday night at ten o'clock. Mr. Noble would be there then and he'd look it over. The boy was driving an old green sedan and when he left, Endicott took down the registration number."

Kay took off his cap and scratched his head. "Did the boy see him do that?"

"That's what we don't know," Paris said. "It's possible the boy saw him through the rear-view mirror. Now Endicott did nothing about this Saturday and Sunday. But on Monday morning we know he left here and went into Eastern City. We don't know if he looked up this registration number. But Monday evening he called the State Police and told them the whole story. He said the boy was supposed to come back that night at ten o'clock. Endicott had a .357 Smith and Wesson Magnum revolver in the desk drawer of his library. But he also wanted a cop there for protection. He was an Endicott, so they sent their best man. That was Lieutenant Hallmark."

"I don't understand it," Kay said. "I'm the police here. Why didn't he call me?"

"I don't know that," Paris said. "But he didn't. Hallmark left his office at the Waretown County Courthouse at eight-thirty. It took him twenty minutes to get to the Endicott house. He was found dead fifteen minutes later. During that time no car was seen or heard driving up to the Endicott house. Not until you and Coats came."

"Then Coyne is right," Kay said. "That boy was in the boat.

He came by water, killed both of them and took the boat back. He had seen Mr. Charles take down the registration number of his car. He cased the house for a couple of days, then he came an hour earlier last night. I've heard about those baby-faced killers. They could do a job like that and eat a ham sandwich at the same time."

"And I've seen them too," Paris said. "That's the most logical way of looking at it and part of it might be right. Because there were a half-dozen rowboats tied up at the wharf of Sunset Harbor and the killer could have used any one of them."

"Those boats belong to the cabin cruisers in the basin," Kay said. "Whose boat did he use?"

"A Mr. Fred Lincoln's," Paris said. "Coyne sent a man over to the wharf. They found one of the motors was warm. But it was wiped clean of prints."

"I know Mr. Lincoln," Kay said. "A fine man. He owns the Lincoln Manufacturing Company and he's had a summer home here for fifteen years."

"I'll go along with that too," Paris said. "The killer just happened to pick his boat. They think the gun used is the one that was in the desk drawer, the .357 Magnum. That's missing. From the type of the wounds, it was a power weapon. A Magnum is a gun with tremendous shock power. They've got the bullets and they're calibrating them now at the lab. But without the gun, the micrometer reading isn't much good. Bullets lose their shape once they're fired."

"I figured everything was scientific now," Kay said.

"Up to a point," Paris said. "Well, that's the story to date, Chief." He stood up and looked at the Endicott house. "Right now I'd like to talk to Mrs. Endicott. Would you come with me?"

"I sure would," Kay said. "So far I ain't been of much use around here. There's troopers all around asking questions, but nobody's told me to do anything. I sure want to help. I'd known Mr. Charles for a long time and I never knew a finer boy. It kind of hurts inside."

"I know," Paris said. "I've got the same hurt."

"And something else keeps bothering me," Kay said.

"What's that?" Paris asked, walking with him toward the entrance of the house.

"You're up against a killer who ain't afraid of cops," Kay said. "He's killed one cop already, and he was a good one. That's why you'd better watch yourself, Inspector. You come too close to him and he'll try to get you too."

3

THEY WENT UP THE BROAD PORTICO, PAST THE STATE trooper on guard there, and rang the bell. They stepped inside. The foyer was dim and cool. Near the door there was a large inlaid wood table with a silver card tray on it. The rug was deep, rich and Oriental. There were chairs with gilt legs and high backs, finished in tapestry. To their left was the wide staircase. The newel post was intricately carved mahogany, the balusters shiny with polish.

At the far end of the hall a door opened. A woman, middle-aged and thin, came down to meet them. She was wearing a gray starched uniform with white collar and cuffs. Her face was worn and tired, her eyes swollen red.

"Elizabeth," Kay said to her, "you've been crying."

"All these years with Mr. Charles," the woman said. "I watched him grow up. That boy was more like a son to me."

"We all watched him grow," Gus Kay said. "That's the sad part of it." He put his hand up and pinched the skin between his eyes. "Well, this is Inspector Paris, Elizabeth. Inspector, Elizabeth Davis. She's the housekeeper here. We've been friends twenty years or more."

"This policeman is a young one, Gus," Elizabeth Davis said to him. "They're all so much younger these days."

"The Inspector is young, but he's good," Kay said. "You'll see."

She looked at Paris. "I suppose you'll be wanting to see my husband Henry too."

"Yes," Paris said. "It would save time."

"I'll fetch him," she said. She left the foyer. Paris, moving near to the wall, touched a large black-onyx pedestal with a carved ivory figure on it.

"Antique," Kay said to him. "You'll see a lot of them around here."

"I'd like to look at the library first," Paris said.

"It's down this way," Kay said.

Paris followed him down a carpeted hallway. There was a massive, burled-walnut door. Kay stopped, opened it gingerly.

The library was big. There was a large walnut flat-topped desk, and a high-backed leather chair behind it. Along one side was a large fireplace with a woven-mesh fire screen. Above the black marble mantel there was an oil painting in a gilt frame, the picture of a man with a calm, serene face and a white Vandyke beard.

Along the back of the room there were two large windows and a glass door, affording a view of the ocean. Paris moved across the room and opened the door. He stepped out. There was a tiled terrace with a filigreed iron railing and it ran the length of the house. Paris went by the leather-and-chrome chaise longues and over to the edge of the railing. Looking down he saw the eroded bluff, the rocks piled beneath it. A pair of stone jetties extended out into the water. Between them was a small sandy beach, and on it, directly below the bluff, was a yellow-striped canvas cabana. To his left was the steel-and-concrete stairway that led down to the dock. Tied to the pier, and rising and falling with the ground swell, was a mahogany-trimmed runabout with a canvas-covered outboard.

Paris turned and went inside again. Chief Kay was standing in the middle of the library, his face set and thoughtful.

"What else leads onto the terrace?" Paris asked him.

"The living room and the dining room," Kay said.

"What about the glass door? Was it locked when you got here?"

"No. It was wide-open. I remember that."

"Is there a wall safe here?"

"Yes."

"Anything missing?"

"No. I heard Mrs. Endicott tell Coyne that. It wasn't tampered with."

Paris went over to the desk. "Were any of these drawers open?"

"No. But that's where Mr. Charles kept the Magnum revolver."

Paris turned around. He walked ten feet across the floor and bent down to the broad, dark stains in the middle of the Oriental rug. "And this is where the bodies were? Ten feet from the desk?"

"Yes," Kay said. He pointed. "Mr. Charles was laying here. Hallmark's body was kind of twisted, and facing toward the opposite wall."

"Face down?"

"Yes."

"Where was his right hand?"

Kay took off his cap and rubbed the back of his head. "Under his coat."

"Near his gun?"

"Yes. I guess he did make a try for it."

"Coyne said Mr. Endicott's wallet was on the floor. Where was that?"

"Right near the body."

"The wallet was open," Paris said. "There was over five hundred dollars in there and it wasn't touched. Something else was taken."

"That's what I figured," Kay said. "The slip of paper with the car registration on it."

"Yes," Paris said. He straightened up. He went over to the walnut door and tried the Yale-type lock. "And this door was locked?"

"No," Kay said. "It was open when Coats and I got here. Henry Davis was standing in front of it."

"You mean the handyman? Elizabeth's husband?"

"Yes."

Paris looked at the top of the desk, at the gray smudges of fingerprint powder, the handset dial telephone. "No prints anywhere," he said. "Everything was deliberately wiped clean. That would take time, at least a minute or two. The killer knew his way around. After all, there were people in this house."

"Yes," Kay said. "He wasn't in no hurry."

"All right," Paris said. "Let's go in and talk to the Davises."

They were waiting for him when he came into the foyer, Mr. Davis, a head shorter than his wife, wearing an open-throated tan shirt, tan trousers and heavy army shoes. His face and hands were sunburnt and his thin gray hair was combed carefully across his head.

Paris acknowledged the introduction, shaking hands with Davis, feeling the strength of his grip. He said, "Now tell me what happened last night, Mr. Davis."

Davis looked at his wife. His wife said, "Henry isn't much for talking. It's better I start it."

"All right," Paris said to her. "You tell it."

"Mr. Charles sent us to bed early," she said. "Eight-thirty, I think. Is that right, Henry?"

Mr. Davis bobbed his head.

"Eight-thirty," Mrs. Davis said. "Mr. Charles said he was expecting visitors and he didn't want anybody around."

"Did he tell you who they were?"

"Yes. He said a state detective was coming. Also a young man with a statue."

"You didn't see any of them arrive?"

"Yes. About ten minutes to nine we heard a car turn into the driveway. I looked out the window of my room. It was an ordinary black sedan. A big husky man came out and went into the house."

"That was Lieutenant Hallmark," Paris said. "You didn't see the young man come?"

"No, sir. I didn't hear any more cars."

"All right," Paris said. "So you went to bed. Then what happened?"

"We didn't go to bed," Mrs. Davis said. "We were in our room. Then we heard some shots. Three of them."

"What time was that?"

"Nine o'clock. I know because we have a chime clock on our mantel and it had just stopped sounding. We weren't sure they were shots either. Sometimes when the boats go out from the basin, and they come by the Point, and they're not warmed up properly, they backfire."

"Why didn't you think this was backfire?"

"Because the sound was kind of muffled. Like from the inside of the house. On the water they sound louder. That's why I told Henry to go down and see."

Paris turned to Mr. Davis. "What did you find?"

Davis, his hands tightly clenched, unclasped them. "The library door was locked, and there was a funny smell like gunpowder. I knocked on the door and I called out for Mr. Charles. But there was no answer. So I went upstairs and told Elizabeth."

"Yes," his wife said. "I told him to get the master key and I went back downstairs with him. He unlocked the door."

"Yes, sir," Davis said. "They were in there, dead. On the floor. They looked terrible, sir."

"You didn't touch anything?"

"No, sir," Davis said. "We didn't go into the room. Elizabeth told me to stand at the door and she went into the hallway to phone the Chief."

"And you did that?" Paris asked her.

"Yes, sir," she said. "I dialed the operator and told her to get Chief Kay. I said Mr. Charles and another man were dead."

"You didn't use the telephone in the library?"

"We didn't go into the library. I wouldn't have gone in there for all the money in the world."

"What did you do after you made the phone call?"

"I ran to get Mrs. Endicott."

"Where was she?"

"She was taking her evening walk. Just like clockwork she is. She leaves at eight-thirty, circles the grounds once, and comes back at nine-thirty."

"Every night?"

"Yes, sir. Even if it rains. Mrs. Endicott is a great believer in walks."

"And where did you find Mrs. Endicott?"

"Just outside the house, sir. She had heard the shots too. She was running toward me. I wouldn't let her in the library. I took her upstairs to her room. And I stayed with her until nine-thirty, when Mr. Noble came."

"According to Lieutenant Coyne's report," Paris said, "you saw a boat going by the bluff. You didn't recognize who was in it?"

"No, sir. It was pitch-dark. I saw the boat. It had its outboard going full blast. It wasn't Mr. Charles's boat because that was at the dock. This boat was heading in toward the basin. I couldn't see who was in it."

"And where was Mr. Endicott's fiancée this whole time?"

"Miss Wyman was out," she said. "She had left at eight o'clock."

"With whom?"

"Mr. Almieda. He's the artist friend of Mr. Charles. He called for her."

"Did Mr. Almieda come in a car?"

"Yes. He has a little convertible."

"And after Mr. Almieda left with Miss Wyman, the next car you heard was the black sedan of Lieutenant Hallmark. Is that right?"

"Yes."

"There were no other cars until Chief Kay arrived?"

"No, sir."

"All right," Paris said. "Thank you, Mrs. Davis. Would you know if Mrs. Endicott is available?"

"She's in the living room with Mr. Hanft," she said. "I'll go and see, sir."

She left. Mr. Davis shifted his feet, looked at them apologetically, and moved out toward the front entrance. Paris and Kay waited. A man opened a door and came into the foyer. He was a tall man. He had curly gray hair, a high forehead with a tan on it, an ascetic face. He was wearing a beige-colored tropical-worsted suit, a white shirt and a dark tie. His wing-toed cordovan shoes were highly polished.

"My name is George Hanft," the man said, putting his hand out to Paris. "I'm the Endicott attorney. Mrs. Endicott will see you. She's quite composed now, but there have been a lot of questions. I wouldn't talk to her too much, Inspector."

"I won't," Paris said. "I'll be as brief as possible."

Paris followed the attorney into the living room, with Chief Kay close behind. There was a huge Regency sideboard along one wall. Over it was a large oil painting of Sunset Point, the big white house, and a wind-whipped sea. The room was long and wide, the ceiling, beamed wood. There were round-seated needlework chairs, bigger chairs in rich tapestry. At the back of the room were large square windows. French doors led to the terrace.

A woman sat on a brocaded oval sofa. She had gray, shingled hair that was swept back on one side and secured with a jeweled clip. She was wearing a dark dress without ornamentation. Her face was long, thin and bloodless, and her mouth was small and tightly drawn.

Mr. Hanft said, "Martha, this is Detective-Inspector Paris. You know the Chief, of course."

Mrs. Endicott nodded slightly. She motioned them to sit down. They remained standing. Kay scuffed his foot on the thick pile of the rug and twisted his cap in his hands. He said, "Mrs. Endicott, the whole town is awful sorry about what hap-

pened to Mr. Charles. Eddie Hansen wants to get up a com-
mittee to pay their respects."

"Thank you, Gus," Mrs. Endicott said evenly. "That's very
thoughtful. I'm grateful to all of you." She looked up at Paris
standing there. "So you're the inspector. Why, you're no older
than Charles was. How old are you really?"

"Thirty-four, Mrs. Endicott."

"A year younger than Charles," she said. "But you carry yourself well. I like that in a man. I wish Charles had taken better
care of his body. He had a tendency to thicken around the
waist."

Paris said, "I know you've been under a strain, Mrs. Endicott.
So I'm not going to take up too much of your time. I thought
possibly you could tell me a few things that would help us."

She looked down at her hands. "I've answered a great many
questions. Your commissioner was here. He's a pompous old
fool and nothing more than a political charlatan. With him was
a very mediocre officer, a Lieutenant Coyne. I know now how big
a price we pay for mediocrity. I've lost my son on account of it."

"No, Mrs. Endicott," Paris said. "Not because of that."

"Naturally you wouldn't say so. Policemen are notorious for
defending their own, no matter how bad or incompetent. Now
you're going to ask questions. You're going to start like they
did. By asking me if my son had any enemies."

"Yes," Paris said.

"Charles had no enemies," she said wearily. "I can't ever conceive of Charles having enemies. He was a quiet, soft-spoken boy
and he was engrossed in the museum. He's the youngest trustee
the museum ever had."

"He left a considerable estate," Paris said. "Who inherits it?"

"Now wait, Martha," Hanft said quickly. "You don't have to
answer that."

"Stop it, George," Mrs. Endicott said. "Don't be so damned
eager to protect my interests. My son has been murdered and
I want his killer brought to justice as swiftly as possible. Nothing
is sacrosanct when it comes to that. Tell the boy."

Hanft looked down at the rug for a moment. His eyes came up and scanned Paris. "When Mr. Charles, Senior, died, he left a large trust fund to Mrs. Endicott. The residue of the estate went to his son, Charles, Junior. Now that Mr. Charles was unmarried and without heirs the entire estate will revert to Mrs. Endicott."

"In other words nobody benefits financially from his death," Paris said.

"Hardly," Hanft said. "Mrs. Endicott already has more than enough for the remainder of her life. There will be some large charitable bequests. But they're secret, of course."

Paris, preoccupied, nodded. He walked over near the sideboard and stood under the oil painting. He examined the scrawled signature of Walter Almieda underneath.

"This Walter Almieda," Paris said. "How friendly was your son with him, Mrs. Endicott?"

"They met in college. Walter came from a poor family, but he was very clever. He went to Harvard on scholarships. Are you a Harvard man, Inspector?"

"No, Mrs. Endicott. I went to State."

"I see," Mrs. Endicott said. "It really makes no difference. Charles went into the Navy during the war. He served as a flag officer in the Pacific. Walter Almieda stayed home, doing poster work for the Army. What did you do, Inspector? Did you stay home too?"

"No," Paris said briefly. "I was a captain in the Infantry."

"I'm sorry," Mrs. Endicott said. "I seem to have misjudged you. Perhaps you're not like your colleagues after all. I know I must have sounded very bitter. You have my apologies, Inspector."

"No," Paris said. "I understand. But I would like to know more about your son and Walter Almieda."

"Charles was a great deal like his father," she said, "in his interest in art and research. My son became attached to Walter Almieda. He gave Walter money to further his career. He sent

Walter to France. He had Walter's paintings exhibited and bought many himself. He saw that his friends bought them. You see, Charles worshipped art. Too much. He had no time for anything else. His father loved art, but he loved life too. His father was different. There was romance in him."

"How did Walter Almieda feel toward your son?"

"What reciprocation Walter showed, I don't know. Personally, I think Walter is a hard, calculating young opportunist. And I think he would use Charles as much as he could. But I might be saying that with prejudice."

"I take it you don't like Mr. Almieda," Paris said.

"No, I don't."

"Then there's Miss Wyman," Paris said. "She was engaged to your son."

"Yes," Mrs. Endicott said. "I never interfered with Charles's personal affairs. My son couldn't judge people. He had no knack at all for earthly things. But I didn't interfere. He met Karen Wyman when she was secretary to Victor Konstanz, the art dealer. She made a show of being interested in art. And because of that Charles became interested in her. What Karen was really interested in, I have a good idea. But it wasn't art. I can't say I was fond of her, Inspector."

"Where is she now?"

"She was at Almieda's cottage last night," Chief Kay said. "I don't know if she's come back."

"She's still at Walter Almieda's," Mrs. Endicott said. "There's the answer to some of her interests, Inspector."

"Thank you," Paris said. He turned to Mr. Hanft. "Counsellor," he said, "how well do you know the Lincolns?"

"Very well," Hanft said. "We've been neighbors here at the beach for twelve years. I do corporation work for Fred Lincoln."

"I notice from Lieutenant Coyne's report that the Lincolns were at your house last night. Who else was there, Counsellor?"

"My wife and Lincoln's son and daughter-in-law."

"What time did they get there?"

"About eight-thirty. We sat down to play cards at nine."

"It's important I establish the exact time," Paris said. "I'd like to pin it down if I can."

"It was exactly nine when we started the card game. That can be verified. Because a minute before then I was talking on the telephone to John Noble. He spoke only briefly to me, but I was impatient and I kept looking at my watch."

"What was the conversation about?"

"Nothing important. It was about the storage pieces. Noble is the curator of the Endicott Collection."

"What storage pieces?"

"The Endicotts have a large collection," Hanft said. "Most of it is on exhibit at the Eastern City Museum. Some of the pieces are on loan to other museums. But there are many objects that have been shown and withdrawn. They're in storage at the museum. The Endicotts pay a personal property tax on them. As long as they're not being shown, I suggested that we sell them, or donate them somewhere. I had talked to Mr. Noble about it and he had agreed with me."

"What about Mr. Endicott? How did he feel about it?"

"He disagreed with us. He said they had belonged to his father and now they were part of the family estate. It was a matter of sentiment. He said he would continue to pay the tax."

"So that closed the matter?"

"Yes, as far as I was concerned. It was my duty to inform him on tax problems. I informed him. He made the decision."

"Then why did Mr. Noble call you?"

"He had a duplicate of the inventory. Mr. Noble is very exacting and fussy about his work. His whole life revolves around the museum. He wanted to know if the matter was closed so he could return the inventory list to his files. I said yes."

"All right," Paris said. "There's one thing more. Mr. Endicott wasn't here all day yesterday. Does anybody know where he went?"

"Yes," Hanft said. "We all knew he went into Eastern City to try to look up the young man and find out something about him. Mr. Charles had the car registration on a slip of paper in his wallet. Nobody knows what information he did find."

Paris turned to Mrs. Endicott. "Did he tell you anything, Mrs. Endicott?"

"No," she said. "He came home about six in the evening and he looked disturbed. He told me he was calling in the State Police. He didn't tell me more."

"And you knew about this Chinese statue?" Paris asked her.

"Yes. We all knew. It was no secret. We had everybody in for cocktails Sunday afternoon and Charles told them all about it."

"And everybody knew he had a gun in his desk drawer?"

Hanft adjusted his shirt collar. "We all knew about the gun," he said. "That was no secret either. The Point is rather isolated. It was necessary to keep a firearm in the house."

"But why did he call the State Police?" Paris asked. "Why didn't he call on Chief Kay? He's the local peace officer."

"I can answer that," Mrs. Endicott said. She looked over at the Chief and smiled wanly. "Gus isn't a young man, and Charles was always very fond of him. If there was any possible danger he didn't want Gus to get hurt."

Kay scuffed the rug. "Now, Mrs. Endicott," he said. "I sure would have wanted to be here. That was my job."

"I know," she said to him. "And that's just the reason Charles didn't want you here. He thought too much of you, Gus. He thought of asking young Coats first. But then he decided it would call for a more experienced man. So he called the State Police. They sent over Lieutenant Hallmark. Possibly that was wrong. Lieutenant Hallmark is dead, and I'm sending a check to his widow because I feel a personal responsibility. But that doesn't alter the fact that the lieutenant was mediocre too. You see, he failed."

"No," Paris said. "Lieutenant Hallmark wasn't mediocre. He was an honest, courageous and experienced policeman. I know because I worked with him many times."

"You're very loyal to his memory," Mrs. Endicott said. "It's an admirable trait. But you can see how ineffective he was. He wasn't capable of coping with a young baby-faced hoodlum half his age."

The room was silent. The air seemed heavy, depressed. "That's what's wrong," Paris said. "Lieutenant Hallmark was shot in the back. That part means a lot to me, Mrs. Endicott. Hallmark would never turn his back on a stranger in a time like that. Nor would he have allowed the boy to get behind the desk. He had been a policeman seventeen years. He would have known better."

"But he did do it," she said.

"I don't know," Paris said. "We're theorizing. Possibly the young man wasn't there. Or if he was there, he wasn't alone. There might have been somebody else with him. And that somebody else might have been a person your son knew and trusted. And because of that Lieutenant Hallmark was reassured. Then this person could have got behind the desk and Hallmark wouldn't have thought anything of it."

"In other words," Hanft said, "you think it might be an inside job. You're not saying that merely to protect Hallmark's name?"

"No," Paris said, "I'm not. I'm looking at it logically. So far all I have is a supposition and I may be entirely wrong. The important thing is the slip of paper with the car registration. You didn't see it?"

"I saw the slip," Hanft said. "Charles showed it. But he didn't show the numbers."

"All right," Paris said. "Mr. Endicott could have gone into the Bureau of Motor Registration Monday and looked up this license number. He could have written down the owner's name and address on the slip of paper. Last night somebody wanted that slip of paper so badly, he murdered two people because of it."

"That sounds reasonable," Hanft said.

"It does," Paris said. "And then again it's pure speculation.

But this is no time to be looking for a scapegoat. Let's bring in the murderer first, then look to see where the blame is."

"And you'll bring in this murderer?" Mrs. Endicott asked.

"I don't know," Paris said. "We're going to try. I'm very sorry about your son's death, Mrs. Endicott. I know being sorry doesn't mean anything. But I *am* sorry."

"Thank you," Mrs. Endicott said. "And I'm sorry if I cast any reflection on Lieutenant Hallmark. But there's one thing more, Inspector. I don't care to have a guard at my front door."

"I'll see he's removed," Paris said. "But I'd advise keeping a guard down the road at the entrance posts. Otherwise you'll be bothered by curiosity seekers."

Hanft nodded. "That would be wise, Martha. These things usually bring out the morbid."

"Very well," Mrs. Endicott said. "It makes little difference. I'm planning to close up and go back to the city." She turned to the windows and looked out to the sea. Her voice was flat and toneless. "You see, I have nothing here now. Nothing at all."

4

THEY CAME ALONG THE BEACH ROAD, PARIS BEHIND THE wheel of the State Police car, beside him, Chief Kay, cap off, the perspiration wetting his forehead. They drove by the large houses, with their slanting seawalls, their bordering green hedges, the striped awnings covering the patios. The houses gave way to smaller ones. There were stretches of empty road and drifts of sand over the asphalt.

This was a small, brown cottage with a red, shingled roof. It stood at the far end of the beach, on a small knoll with a green expanse of lawn in front of it. There was a row of flagstones that led up to the house and to the screened porch. On the road below was a small blue convertible, top down, one tire badly worn.

"This is Almieda's car," Kay said, as Paris parked behind it. "And this is the Almieda cottage. Well, it ain't really his cottage. He's been renting it. But he gets a good view of the Point from here. You wait until you see this Karen Wyman. Fluffy blonde, blue eyes. And she ain't society either. She's got some shape too. Came down the beach one day in one of those Bikini bathing suits. I didn't know whether to run her in for indecent exposure or go after my camera and get a picture of her. I did neither. I just stood there goggle-eyed."

Paris smiled. He stepped out of the car. Above, the door of the screened porch opened and a man stood there. Paris went up the flagstones behind Chief Kay. They came up to the short step leading to the porch. The man looked down at them. He was tall and heavily framed. His dark hair was unkempt and the beginning of a beard darkened his skin. He was wearing a wide-ribbed orange sport shirt, pale-blue slacks, and blue suede shoes with rope laces.

"What's this?" the man asked. "Another inquisition?"

Kay grunted. "This is Detective-Inspector Paris," he said. "He wants to talk to you and Miss Wyman, Mr. Almieda."

"What makes you think she's here?" Almieda asked.

"Well, she didn't come back to the Endicott house," Kay said. "I guess she couldn't be any place else."

Almieda swung the door open. "Come in," he said. "Let's get it over with."

They went up the step and onto the porch. The floor boards were painted gray. There were a square fiber mat, a plastic-covered glider and two wicker chairs. The glass-topped wicker table held two empty highball glasses and a brass ashtray filled with lipstick-smeared cigarette butts. Paris looked away, watching the sun glint off the water, his eyes toward the Point where the big white house was slightly obscured in the heat haze.

"Let's talk out here," Paris said. "It's cooler." He turned his head to Almieda. "Would you call Miss Wyman?"

"I didn't say she was here," Almieda said.

"Come now," Kay said to him. "No sense getting all fussed

up. We ain't talking about the lady's reputation. The Inspector wants to ask a few questions, that's all."

The door to the house opened and a girl stepped out. She had a high, full bosom. Her body was soft and shapely, her skin a golden tan. She had blonde hair and a childlike round face. Her eyes were large and blue. She was wearing a strapless black-rayon cocktail gown, and there was a rhinestone chain attached to it that circled her upper left arm. Her legs were slim and nylon-sheathed. She was wearing black cutaway pumps with very high heels.

Kay took off his cap. "Miss Wyman," he said, "this is Inspector Paris."

She looked carefully at Paris and smiled. "How do you do, Inspector? I must look frightful this time of day. I'm sorry about my costume. But here I am without a stitch to my name. I was wearing this last night and I couldn't go back to get my clothes."

"Mrs. Endicott was wondering where you were," Kay said.

"I'm not going back there," she said. "I couldn't *stand* going back to that house."

"Why?" Paris asked.

"Now wait a minute," Almieda said. "Don't try to twist her words into things she doesn't mean."

"It's all right, Walter," she said soothingly. "I've nothing to hide."

"Not much," Kay said, looking at the tight, strapless dress. Karen Wyman moved by him with a half-smile, and sat down on the glider. She swung it to and fro gently. Almieda frowned, moved over and sat down beside her. He planted his feet firmly and stopped the motion of the glider. Chief Kay leaned against the screen door, his thumbs through his leather holster belt.

"Maybe you haven't heard of Inspector Paris," Almieda said to Karen Wyman. "He has a reputation for ruthlessness. He once arrested half the Eastern City Police Department. He's a new type of human machine. All science and no blood."

"I don't think we're interested in your opinions now," Paris said mildly. "I'm checking Lieutenant Coyne's report. It says you called for Miss Wyman at eight o'clock last night. Where did you go?"

"We came here," Almieda said. "Karen was bored. Anyway Charles didn't want her around last night."

"What time did you get here?"

"I don't know," Almieda snapped. "Everybody asks me the same question. I didn't time it. If you drove here from the Point you'd know it takes about ten minutes."

Kay shifted his body. He said, "What are you so excited about, Mr. Almieda?"

"It's hot," Almieda said. "I'm damn tired of questions."

"That's too bad," Paris said. "I'm hot and tired too. But your friend, Charles Endicott, was murdered last night. That should make a difference to you."

"Don't wave the flag at me," Almieda said.

"All right," Paris said. "How long did you stay here?"

"All evening."

"You were both here alone?"

"Yes."

Paris looked over at Karen Wyman. "Did he leave the cottage at any time, Miss Wyman?"

"No, Inspector. He didn't."

"Did you, Miss Wyman?"

"Oh no."

"You were both here the whole time?"

"What are you getting at?" Almieda asked. "Are you inferring she's lying?"

"I didn't say she was lying," Paris said. "Let her answer the question."

"We were here the whole time," Karen Wyman said.

"Mr. Almieda," Paris said, "do you know how to handle an outboard motor?"

"What's that got to do with it?"

"I'm asking you."

"Yes," Almieda said. "I know how."

"You, Miss Wyman?"

"I've used them."

Paris pulled over a wicker chair and sat down. "How long ago did you become engaged to Charles Endicott, Miss Wyman?"

"Three months ago," she said.

"And how long have you known Walter Almieda?"

"Four weeks, I guess. I met him down here."

"You never knew him before?"

"No."

"For a girl who was engaged to somebody else, aren't you rather intimate with a man you just met?"

Almieda stared at him, color going to his face. He stood up slowly. He faced Paris, his breathing short and rapid. "I've got a good mind to clip you one," he said.

"You'd better sit down," Paris said briefly. "I don't like heroics."

"Please, Walter," Karen Wyman said. "Sit down. Pretty, pretty please?"

Almieda stood there, his hands hanging loosely, his face immobile. He sat down again.

"Paris said, "Are you married, Mr. Almieda?"

"I don't care to talk any more," Almieda said.

"All right," Paris said. "I'll take you along and talk to you somewhere else."

"Don't pout, Walter," Karen Wyman said. "I don't like it when you pout."

"Okay," Almieda said curtly. "I'm not married."

"Were you ever married?"

"Yes."

"How many times?"

"Twice."

"You're divorced now?"

"Yes."

"Tell me," Paris said. "How did you get along with Mrs. Endicott?"

"You're going to discuss my personal affairs?"

"Yes," Paris said. "How did you get along with Mrs. Endicott?"

"I didn't like her," Almieda said. "I never liked her. She was too damn patronizing. I don't like to be patronized, and with my ability, I don't have to stand for it. I told her so. And if you want to know something else, she didn't like me either."

"What about Charles Endicott? Did you like him?"

"Now that's an infantile question. I'd say I liked him anyway. I'm not going to give you any kind of a motive."

"You didn't answer the question," Paris said.

"Of course I liked him. Everybody liked him. Charles was like a big, overgrown spring lamb. We went to school together and he was always around me with those big sheeplike eyes of his. He had no talent himself, so he idolized talent in somebody else. I like adulation, I'll admit it. So, even if Charles *was* a bit on the dull side, I liked him."

"And you, Miss Wyman," Paris said. "How was your relationship with Mrs. Endicott?"

"Oh," she said, her eyes widening innocently. "I tried so hard to make her fond of me. But it *was* a project. She's such a health faddist. She wanted me to take long walks with her. And she insisted I become an amazon of a woman to rear a healthy heir. She said I should eat yogurt and brewers' yeast and blackstrap molasses and wheat germ. Do I look as though I need those things, Inspector?"

"I'm sure I couldn't tell you," Paris said. "You're not presently employed, Miss Wyman?"

"Oh, no. I had discussed it with Charles and he agreed that it wouldn't be proper for an Endicott bride-to-be to have a job." She tilted her head to him and smiled. "So I quit."

"And how about money?" Paris asked.

"Well," she said, "Charles might have been a cold drink of

water. But he didn't think there was anything wrong with my having an allowance to tide me over until the marriage."

"And if he was such a cold drink of water, how much were you in love with him?"

"Oh, isn't that cruel of you," she said in a shocked voice. "Of course I was devoted to Charles. Very much. I would just die if I thought something would happen to him."

"You're a little mixed up," Paris said. "Something did happen to him. And you look like the picture of health."

"You're trying to confuse her," Almieda shouted at him.

"I'm looking for a murderer," Paris said. "Sometimes people say one thing when they mean another. Miss Wyman, you say you were in love with Charles Endicott. How much of it was his position and money?"

"Well, I'd be fibbing if I said I wasn't impressed with that too. Any girl would be."

"But you were bored too. Is that it?"

"Well, Charles was so matter-of-fact about me. It was disconcerting, to say the least. Half the time he didn't know I was around. He was always puttering around that old museum and looking up things in dusty old books." She looked at Almieda with a baby smile and wriggled close to him. "I don't know what I would have done if Walter hadn't come along to amuse me. I thought Charles would surely notice me more then."

"You mean you tried to make him jealous?"

"Now you're trying to read my mind." She giggled. "It didn't work at all. Charles was oblivious to it."

"So there were no quarrels about you?"

"Unfortunately no."

"Did you know Mr. Endicott was expecting a visitor last night?"

"A man was coming to see him about a horse," Almieda said impatiently. "We all knew that. What else do you want to know?"

"Nothing else now," Paris said, getting up. "But as a close friend of Endicott's, I'd expected a little more grief from you."

"I'm very staunch," Almieda said. "I grieve within." He ran his hand through his hair. "But here's something else. There's a little matter Karen is interested in."

"And what's that?"

"This is pure supposition," Almieda said. "But Karen thought that with Charles and her being engaged—and with the marriage being so close and all—that he might have made some sort of provision for her."

"What kind of provision?"

"Well, he could have made some arrangement for her in his will."

"What a terrible thing to bring up," Karen Wyman said. "How can you talk like that, Walter, in front of strangers?"

"I blush for you," Almieda said, "because you're not capable of blushing. It's only a hypothetical question, darling. But perhaps the will has been discussed with the Inspector."

"If it's hypothetical," Paris said, "I'll give you a hypothetical answer. I think you're going to be disappointed, both of you."

He left them, walked down the flagstones to the car. Kay followed him. Paris got in behind the wheel.

"Nice people," Kay said, nodding his head toward the house.

"Yes," Paris said, his face hard and set.

"I wouldn't give a nickel for that Almieda," Kay said, opening the door and getting in. "He looks like he'd take what he could, where he could get it. And he wouldn't keep it long either. How long do you think he'll hold onto Miss Wyman?"

"Until he gets what he can from her," Paris said, putting the car in gear. "But I wouldn't worry about Miss Wyman either. I've got a hunch she's more than a match for him."

5

THERE WAS A WOODEN SIGN ON THE LAWN. THE SIGN, neat, small-lettered, said WHITE SANDS APART-

MENTS. Paris, parking the car there, noticed the old three-story, wood-frame structure, the side fire escapes, the white clapboard and the black trim. There was a long veranda that ran the length of the building. In the chairs in the shade, the elderly people, their conversation listlessly waning in the heat, looked over at the State Police car.

Paris got out and followed Chief Kay up the stairs to the lobby. Inside there were a large straw rug, scattered white-painted rattan furniture. There was a steep narrow staircase. They went up to the second floor and along the dim narrow corridor to the very end. Kay stopped. The door had the number 12 on it. Kay knocked.

A voice said, "Come in."

The room was simple, clean and small. There was the same white rattan furniture as in the lobby. There were a small table and a lamp. On a stand near the wall there was a dial telephone, on the shelf under it a white plastic clock radio. There was a slip-covered sofa, in front of it a small cocktail table.

A man sat in a rattan rocker, his hands folded in his lap. He had fine-spun white hair and a smooth, bland, pink-cheeked complexion. He was wearing a white nylon sport shirt and striped seersucker trousers. His eyes, looking up at them, were patient and resigned.

"Mr. Noble," Kay said. "This is Detective-Inspector Paris."

Noble stood up and nodded uncertainly. He fluttered his hands. "Please sit down, gentlemen."

Paris moved over and sat down in a chair. Kay leaned against the door.

Noble said, "I've been waiting here all day. They said there would be more questions."

"Now you don't have to stay in your apartment," Kay told him. "They meant for you to be available, Mr. Noble. But you could have gone down to the lobby or the veranda."

"I didn't know," Noble said. "When it comes to the police I'm rather a novice."

Paris looked past the living room to the opened door of the

bedroom. He saw the maple bed, the leather two-suiter bag near it. There was a hatrack with a dark raincoat and a hat on it, and a black umbrella hanging from one of the rungs. On the floor below it was a pair of black rubbers.

"Do you take this apartment for the entire summer?" Paris asked.

"Yes," Noble said, sitting down carefully. "I'm not much for fishing or swimming, but Mr. Charles always liked to have me handy. I could stay at the hotel, of course. But I'm an old bachelor. After all these years, I've acquired a taste for my own cooking, as bad as it is."

"Mr. Noble," Paris said, "last night you spoke over the telephone to Mr. Hanft. Do you remember the exact time?"

Noble pursed his full red lips. "No," he said, "not the exact time. It was about nine o'clock."

"And what did you speak to Mr. Hanft about?"

"The inventory on the storage pieces. I asked Mr. Hanft if it was proper to put the list back in my files. I keep very good files, you know. I've been at the museum twenty-six years. I know exactly where everything is."

"Is this a large inventory?"

"Yes. It's quite a large inventory for a private collection."

"And it runs into a considerable sum of money?"

"Oh yes. But the market would vary according to the demand."

"In other words," Paris said, "Mr. Endicott could have realized a large amount of cash if he had sold these surplus pieces."

"Yes. But Mr. Charles was never interested in money. He never had particular occasion to worry about money."

Paris took out a pack of cigarettes and offered them around. Chief Kay came over and took one. Mr. Noble smiled shyly and refused.

Paris lit up and blew the smoke from his mouth. The room temperature was warm. He loosened his collar. He said, "Mr. Endicott spoke to you about a Chinese horse that was offered to him. When was that?"

"Last Friday evening. He spoke to me about it Sunday too.

I went back to Eastern City to get the equipment to examine it."

"When was that, Mr. Noble?"

"Yesterday. I returned in the afternoon."

"Last Friday, when the young man came with this horse, you didn't see him?"

"No."

"We're a little desperate for a description of him," Paris said. "He might have had a record and his picture could be on file."

"I know. I'm terribly sorry, sir. And I would like to help. But I think Mr. Charles saw him alone."

"Last night," Paris said, "you were supposed to come to the house to examine this horse. Is that right?"

"Yes, sir," Noble said. "That was in the event the young man came."

"You didn't think he would come?"

"I'm afraid not. I thought he would become frightened. But Mr. Charles insisted the young man would be there. He asked me to come at nine-thirty. The young man was supposed to come at ten."

"Did he tell you the State Police would be there?"

"Yes. He called me earlier and said an officer was coming over."

"And you arrived at nine-thirty?"

"Yes, sir. When I got to the house I saw Chief Kay there." He paused. His pink face trembled. "It was a tremendous blow to me, sir. A tremendous blow. I've known Mr. Charles since he was a child. He was such a splendid young man. It will be a great tragedy to the museum. He was a trustee, you know."

"Yes," Paris said. "Now, you drove over to the Endicott house at nine-thirty. Did you see anything unusual on the way?"

"No, sir. I saw nothing unusual."

"All right," Paris said. "Now what about this Chinese horse? How would you have determined if it was genuine?"

"Well," Noble said, "Mr. Charles was under the impression

that it was an authentic T'ang Dynasty piece about twelve inches high. If it was T'ang, it would be made of pottery, not porcelain. Porcelain didn't come into use until later. We could analyze the composition of the clay by chemical reaction. That would give us a good idea."

"Do you have any T'ang horses at the museum now?"

"No, sir."

"Mr. Endicott never owned one?"

"No. We do have a T'ang camel. A large piece about twenty-six inches. But it doesn't have blue-lead glaze. Mr. Charles said this horse had blue splashes."

"Would that make the horse more valuable?"

"Yes. Blue glaze was extremely rare in the T'ang period."

"And what would this horse be worth?"

"You mean in money?"

"Yes."

"I can't venture a guess on that," Noble said, shaking his head. "It depends on the market, and how badly Mr. Charles wanted it. We usually don't place a monetary value on museum pieces."

"Would ten thousand dollars be a fair price?"

"Yes, if Mr. Endicott wanted it to round out the collection. I think it's not an unfair price."

"Do you think the horse was stolen from somewhere?"

"I couldn't say, sir. There's no report of a T'ang horse disappearing. It's possible the horse *might* have been obtained by illegal means. Then again, a piece like that could turn up anywhere."

"But a man would have to know something of Asiatic art. This young man set a price of ten thousand dollars on it. He must have had an idea of the value."

"Yes, I think that's logical."

Paris snuffed out his cigarette in the small ceramic ashtray. He stood up. "Mr. Noble," he said, "where did Mr. Endicott go yesterday?"

"I can tell you that," Noble said. "He told me he was going into Eastern City to look up the car registration of the young man. He was going to make an attempt to trace him down. I tried to dissuade him. I thought the police should handle such matters. But how Mr. Charles actually went about it, I don't know." He smiled diffidently. "I wanted to go with him. I had to be in the museum anyway. But he said he wanted to do it alone."

Paris said, "Do you know an art dealer named Victor Konstanz?"

"Oh yes," Noble said. "We've transacted business with Victor Konstanz for many, many years."

"You know, of course, that Miss Wyman worked for Mr. Konstanz."

"Yes. She did until a few months ago. That was when Mr. Charles met her. It blossomed into romance. I was glad for Mr. Charles." He smiled faintly. "I despaired that he'd end up an old bachelor like myself, with only the museum to count for his existence."

"Would you know of any friction?" Paris asked. "I mean, would there be any reason for Mr. Konstanz to have animosity toward Charles Endicott because of that? Jealousy, for example?"

A pair of pale-blue eyes came up and stared at him. "Oh, I can't conceive of that. Mr. Konstanz is not a young man. I think he's been happily married for over thirty-five years. No, it could be nothing like that."

"I thought I'd ask," Paris said.

"I understand. It's necessary to explore every realm of possibility."

"Yes," Paris said. "Thank you, Mr. Noble. I think that's all for now. And you don't have to stay in your apartment. If we need you, we'll know where you are."

"Thank you, Inspector," Noble said. He stood up, hesitated and looked over at the door. "I thought I'd go over and sit with Mrs. Endicott, if I may."

"That will be all right," Paris said. "You give your name to the guard at the entrance. I'll call up and see that he lets you through."

Paris picked up his hat. Chief Kay opened the door and they went out. They walked down the narrow stairway to the lobby.

"Five o'clock," Kay said, looking at his strap watch. "The day went by fast."

They went out onto the veranda. Kay stopped. "This building is old," he said, tapping the clapboard wall. "It was once called the Silver Strand Hotel. When Eddie Hansen bought it he put kitchens in and converted it into tiny apartments. But you don't know these old summer hotels. Those walls are as thin as tissue paper and Hansen wasn't going to spend any more money insulating them. You only get a short season here, and he'd have to tear the whole place down.

"I'll tell you about these walls. They're so thin you can hear ordinary conversation between the apartments. When folks complain to Hansen he tells them they're only here a short time and that it makes the place friendlier anyway. Besides, if anybody has anything to hide from his neighbors he shouldn't come here. That's what Eddie Hansen says."

Paris nodded impatiently and started down the stairs to the car. Kay followed him.

"I'm trying to bring out a point," Kay said. "Take Mr. Noble. He's been coming to Apartment Twelve for six, seven years now. You see that clock radio he had? That radio belongs to Mr. Noble. Eddie don't give radios. He's a guy who's a great believer in not spoiling his guests. Noble's got other things of his own here. In the bedroom there's a portable closet and a hatrack. He's got his own pictures on the wall."

Paris had come to the car. He opened the door and got in. Chief Kay stood at the open window and looked back at the White Sands Apartments.

"We played cards last night," Kay said, "like we do every Monday night. Hansen's apartment is Number Eleven, right next to Noble's. What I'm trying to tell you is that I heard Mr. Noble talking on the telephone last night."

Paris, the car key in his hand, stopped. He stared over at Kay. "You heard what, Chief?"

"I heard him on the telephone."

"What time was that?"

"About a minute before nine o'clock. I told the boys to cut the noise a little so the poor fellow could hear himself talk."

"And he was talking to Mr. Hanft?"

"Yes."

"What were they talking about?"

"Of course, I could only hear Mr. Noble," Kay said. "He was telling Mr. Hanft that he would put the inventory list back in the files and close it. I could hear him through that wall as clear as you're talking to me. They spoke maybe a minute, not more."

Kay opened the door and got in. He settled down in the seat and took out one of his little black cigars. He said, "I guess it boils down to this. It looks like I'm a witness for both Mr. Noble and Mr. Hanft as to where they were at nine o'clock last night. In case you were thinking along those lines."

"I'll admit I was," Paris said. "That's part of the job. Did they say anything about the Chinese horse?"

"I heard every word," Kay said. "The only mention was that Mr. Noble said he was going over to the Endicott house in half an hour." He lit the cigar and blew the smoke thoughfully. "It's a rotten piece of business. While they were talking like that, Mr. Charles was being shot down."

"Yes," Paris said, pressing the starter button. "Well, it looks like we've done all we can here now. Thanks for the co-operation, Chief."

"I should be thanking you," Kay said. "I like the education I'm getting. Where are you planning on going now?"

"It's too late to do anything today," Paris said. "Tomorrow morning I'll have to start looking for a kid with a Chinese horse."

"That's what I thought," Kay said. "You'd better watch yourself when you go up against him."

"Thanks," Paris said. "If I find him."

6

THERE WAS A LOW MORNING CLOUD BANK THAT HUNG
over Eastern City. The air was leaden, warm and humid.
Paris, parking the car at the curb, felt the moisture of his collar
and the dampness of his clothes.

It was one of a group of two-story brownstone houses that
had been converted into business places—among them exclusive
dress shops, an interior decorator, an advertising agency, in-
vestment brokers. This one had two cut-glass chandeliers suspended in the front bay windows. There was an antique iron
sign. The sign, on a chain above the door, said VICTOR
KONSTANZ GALLERIES. Paris passed under it, went up the
stairs and inside.

A man came forward to greet him—a tall, thin young man,
slightly stooped, wearing heavy horn-rimmed glasses, his suit
blue and chalk-striped.

"Is Mr. Konstanz in?" Paris asked.

"Whom shall I say is calling?"

Paris told him. The man said, "If you'll excuse me a
moment—"

He went away quickly. Paris waited, noticing the large tapes-
tries suspended from the walls, the ornate, gleaming, sterling-
silver serving pieces on velvet-covered tables, the flowered
China vases. The man came back.

"Mr. Konstanz will see you in his office," he said. He pointed.
"It's upstairs, sir."

There was a wide, carpet-covered staircase. Paris went up.
At the top of the stairs there was a large darkened showroom.
To the left of it was a small, glass-paneled door. Paris opened it.

The room was small. There was a huge wall safe with two old-fashioned dials on it. In front there was an old rolltop desk. A man rose from behind it. The man was short and portly. He had a fat face and pouched eyes. He was almost completely bald, a few white hairs on either side of his temples. He put out his hand. Paris reached and took it. It was soft and flabby.

"Sit down, sir," Mr. Konstanz said, motioning to a chair. "My Mr. Jelkes told me you were a State Police Inspector."

"Yes," Paris said. He took out his leather folder and showed the blue-and-silver shield.

"That's quite all right," Konstanz said, nodding his head. "It's only because you look so young."

Paris sat down. "I wanted to talk to you about Charles Endicott," he said.

"A most terrible tragedy," Konstanz said sadly. "A most terrible tragedy. Everybody is very upset. I phoned Mrs. Endicott immediately to offer my poor services. She was unavailable, poor soul." He put up his hand and rubbed his fat jowls. "Mr. Charles will be a great loss, a great loss. We can ill afford to lose the few generous patrons we have. Do you have any idea who the culprit might be, Inspector?"

"That's why I came to see you," Paris said. "Was Mr. Endicott here Monday?"

"Yes. And I was going to call the police about it. I thought it might have some bearing on the case."

"What time Monday was he here?"

"In the afternoon. He came to ask me about a T'ang horse. He said it had blue splashes. He wanted to know if I knew anything about it."

"Did you?"

"No. I told him I hadn't heard of one recently. But I would have been delighted to get my hands on one like that."

"Did Mr. Endicott go into it further? Did he ask you if anybody had offered you one for sale?"

"Yes," Konstanz said, looking up in surprise. "As a matter of fact, he did. I told him nobody had offered me one. That was all. I showed him some tenth-century Rakka jars and some bronzes by Maillol, but he wasn't interested. He left shortly afterwards."

"He didn't tell you where he was going?"

"No."

"Mr. Konstanz, how long did Karen Wyman work for you?"

Konstanz leaned back in the chair and puckered his lips. "About a year, I think. I can check and find out exactly."

"That won't be necessary. Did she come to you with good references?"

Konstanz chuckled. "I really don't remember. She was so decorative I don't think I inquired. I was sorry to see her go. Karen wasn't very efficient, but she did do so much for the surroundings. Mr. Charles took preference, of course. It wouldn't do to have Mr. Charles's fiancée engaged in trade."

"No, I suppose not," Paris said. "Did Miss Wyman have other admirers?"

Konstanz chuckled again. "We were all her admirers, so to speak. My Mr. Jelkes especially. He was hopelessly in love with her. I daresay he spent his entire salary and drained his bank account trying to amuse her. It was unfortunate. There was no reciprocation. Karen has the most innocent large eyes, and she's childlike. But she's also childlike in her greed. I have an idea her heart is the size of a cherry pit, and just as hard."

"I'd like to talk about this T'ang horse," Paris said. "It was offered to Endicott by a shabby young man. Where could the horse have come from?"

Konstanz put his fat fingers to his lip and his eyes roamed around the tiny office. "Ah, that *is* a question. Where? I'll show you things in my showroom. Lithograph posters by Toulouse-Lautrec, a George Third china cabinet, Persian swords, Georgian silver, Roman and Greek antiquities, carved jade table screens. Where do they come from you ask? Anywhere. This T'ang horse? It could have been stolen from somebody. It could have been picked up for a few dollars at an auction. It could have come off some ship, in a seaman's duffle bag. Those pieces some-times turn up in the most unusual places."

"Origins," Paris said. "These objects have origins. Where did the horse first come from?"

"You're really determined to trace it, aren't you?"

"Yes," Paris said. "I'll go back that far if necessary."

"Well, originally, of course, they come from the tombs of the T'ang emporers. They were burial pieces."

"And what are those?"

"Funeral pottery. Seventh and eighth century A.D. But the story starts many, many centuries before that, when it was the custom of the Chinese of high station to practice immolation. When an emperor died, he was supposed to continue to have all his luxuries while he was waiting to be received into the other world. So they would build him an enormous tomb. In there they would bury alive his favorite wives, concubines, servants, horses, food, everything. When K'ung-Fu-tze came along, he preached against it. The Reverend Master K'ung, or Confucius as we call him, was so successful in his persuasions that the practice began to die out. They buried these statues instead. The horse could be the Bactrian type that was introduced into China at that time."

"All right," Paris said. "But these pieces later turned up in America. How? Who brought them? The clipper ships in the China trade?"

"No," Konstanz said. "Later than that. It was after the turn of the century. The first T'ang tombs weren't discovered until about 1906. That was the time China was trying to go modern. They were excavating the roadbeds for their first railroads."

"Who built these railroads?"

"Coolies, of course. But under the supervision of Occidental engineers." Konstanz spread his hands flat on the desk. "There," he smiled. "You've hit on it. Engineers. That's how some of the T'ang horses showed up. A few of them also fell into the hands of missionaries at that time."

"All right," Paris said. "Suppose one of these former engineers or missionaries died. A T'ang piece could show up in the estate."

"Why, yes. They could come to light at an auction or private sale."

"Then this horse could have been bought at an auction," Paris said.

"Yes."

"And it could have been sold without the administrator of the estate knowing the true value of it."

"It happens all the time," Konstanz said. "I could tell you of a hundred cases."

"Now," Paris said. "Were there any auctions recently in this area?"

"Yes. A few. Of course most auctions aren't really estate auctions. They're staged by the antique dealers themselves. They get hold of a house and bring their own things."

"Is that an accepted practice?"

"Oh yes. It's always been done. I go to these auctions myself. Sometimes I pick up something."

"We've been talking about legitimate business," Paris said. "But there are dealers who handle stolen merchandise."

Konstanz compressed his mouth. "We have our unscrupulous dealers, but fewer than any other business."

"I understand that," Paris said. "I want the names of those in this area."

"Do I have to tell you that, Inspector?"

"No, you don't. I'm asking you merely to save time. I could find out in a minute. It would take only a phone call."

"Of course, of course," Konstanz said. "Well, there are two dealers who aren't exactly crooked in the sense of the word. But I don't think they'd check too closely as to the source of the things they buy. Their names are Homer Talmadge and William Lakos."

Paris took out his notebook and wrote the names down. "Now," he said. "When was the most recent auction? Not one that was promoted by dealers, but a real one."

"You mean an estate auction?"

"Yes."

"Last Friday morning," Konstanz said.

Paris sat up in his chair. "You're sure it was last Friday morning?"

"Yes," Konstanz said. "July twentieth. Lester Mann, the auctioneer, handled it. He's the biggest in the city and he'd only handle entire estates. It was an old house in the Mirror Park section." He leaned back in his chair and tilted it. "I'm trying to think of the family name. Kolloway. The Kolloway auction."

"Was Mr. Talmadge there?"

"No, I didn't see him."

"Mr. Lakos?"

"Yes. Lakos was there."

"Did he buy anything?"

"I don't know."

"Was he in company with anybody?"

"I don't think I paid attention."

"A young man," Paris said. "Reddish-blond hair, baby-faced. Was he there?"

Konstanz pulled at his chin and stared down at the desk blotter. "There were a great many people there. It's possible."

"Mr. George Hanft," Paris said. "Was he there?"

"You mean the Endicott attorney?"

"Yes."

"No, I don't remember seeing him."

"How about Mr. Noble?"

"No. John Noble wasn't there. He doesn't usually attend auctions. If the occasion arose, Mr. Charles would go himself."

"But Mr. Endicott didn't go to this one?"

"No."

"How about Walter Almieda?"

Konstanz pursed his mouth and thought for a moment. "I don't think so. He's the artist friend of Mr. Charles?"

"Yes."

"Of course. He does seascapes. I don't know him well. Mr.

Charles asked me to show some of his work once, but I begged off. Some people associate ego with talent."

"All right," Paris said. "And as far as you know, there was no T'ang horse offered at this auction?"

"I'd have jumped up quick if there had been. No. And I didn't stay very long either. Most of the things were Empire and Victorian and rather seedy. And certainly there was no T'ang horse for sale. If there had been, Mr. Mann would have notified me in advance."

"Then I guess that's all," Paris said, standing up. "I'm sorry to have taken up so much of your time."

"That's perfectly all right," Konstanz said. "It's more than worth it if it will turn up the murderer."

"Thanks," Paris said.

He went out, down the staircase, past Mr. Jelkes, and outside to his car.

7

THE SUN HAD BROKEN THROUGH THE CLOUDS, INCREASING the humid heat. There was a cloying smell of hot sidewalks. Paris parked the car in Post Office Square and entered a large gray, soot-smudged building. The offices of the Lester Mann Company were on the sixth floor. The frosted-glass entrance door carried the name and a small red auctioneer's flag.

There was a large, buxom woman at a desk and Paris gave her his name. The woman plugged into a small switchboard and spoke. Mr. Mann came out. He was tall, freckle-faced and middle-aged. He shook hands firmly. Paris went with him across the small center office and into a carpeted, mahogany-furnished room. Mann waved him to a chair.

"Anything I can do, Inspector," he said, "would be a pleasure. How about a drink first? Or do you have prejudices against morning drinking?"

"No, thanks," Paris said. "I'm interested in an auction last Friday. The Kolloway auction. You handled it?"

"Yes, that was mine. Is there anything wrong?"

"I don't know yet," Paris said. "Who were these Kolloways?"

"It was Miss Augusta Kolloway," Mann said, moving behind his desk and sitting down. "She was a maiden lady. The last of the Kolloways. There were no heirs. The house and furnishings went up to satisfy creditors."

"What was the family background?"

"They were old Eastern City folks," Mann said. "Eighty years and more. Church people."

"Missionaries?"

"Yes," Mann said. "But not recently. Years back there were missionaries in the family. The last of them was Miss Augusta's brother."

"Had he been to China?"

"I think so. From some of the letters I found, he had traveled all through the Far East and the South Pacific."

"All right," Paris said. "Now, did you offer anything unusual at the auction?"

"No. The house furnishings were mostly Victorian and a few Empire pieces. There were some haircloth chairs, a couple of marble-topped tables, some lamps with china globes. A few whatnots and odds and ends. Chinaware and silver."

"No antique Chinese figurines?" Paris asked.

"No."

"I'm looking for a T'ang horse," Paris said. "You didn't offer one for sale?"

"Are you kidding, Inspector? T'ang? No. No T'ang, no Han, no Ming or Manchu either. I wish there were."

"Did Mr. Lakos buy anything there?"

"You mean William Lakos?"

"Yes."

"No," Mann said. "I think he made a bid on something, but he didn't stay with it. I don't remember what it was."

"How about Homer Talmadge?"

"Talmadge? No, Talmadge wasn't there. I understand he's been at the Cedar Heights Hospital for three months now. Bad heart condition. Coronary."

"This auction is important to me," Paris said. "Somebody bought something there." He stood up. He went to the window and looked out. The heat waves shimmered off the roofs of the adjoining buildings. The air was still. A flag drooped at its staff. Paris turned around. "Think," he said. "Something that could have been concealed. A box, perhaps. A carton. A chest of drawers with something still in it."

"No," Mann said. "We go through the furniture first." He leaned forward and touched his fingertips together. "No, not a box. There was an old steamer trunk. Does that help you?"

"Yes. What was in it?"

"It was mostly empty. A few curios from the Islands. There was some cheap Japanese tourist junk. I sold it as one lot."

"To whom?" Paris asked.

"Old man Shapp, I think. You want me to check on it?"

"Yes, please."

Mann stood up, went out of the office, leaving the door open. A typewriter clicking, stopped. There was the sound of a drawer opening. Paris waited. Lester Mann came back.

"It was Abe Shapp all right," he said. "He bought it. I knocked it down to him for twenty-five dollars."

"I'll want his address," Paris said.

"It's 163 Somerset Street. He has his place of business there. I think he lives there too. Over the store."

"Thanks," Paris said.

He went out of there quickly, down the elevator and out to the street.

The store was old. The sign, in oxidized paint, said *A. Shapp. Antiques Bought and Sold.* Looking in through the fly-specked window, Paris could see the dusty bric-a-brac; tarnished pewter, a tiny fiddle-backed chair, an old Tower musket, verdigrised and barrel-rusted.

Paris opened the door. A little bell jangled above him. There was an aged musty odor. The narrow shop was crowded with a jumble of furniture.

A girl came out of the shadows. As she came closer, Paris saw she was tall and well-formed. She had golden-red hair, brushed severely back, a skin, soft and satiny. Her mouth was round and full and her eyes, sea-green. She was wearing a short-sleeved, trim white dress with a black braided belt, seamless sheer stockings and French-heeled white doeskin pumps. She wasn't more than twenty-two years old.

"Yes?" she said.

"I'm looking for Mr. Shapp," Paris said.

"He's not here. Is there anything I can do?"

"No, thanks," Paris said. "When will he be back?"

"He's upstairs having his lunch. He should be down in a minute."

"I'll wait," Paris said.

The girl looked at him briefly and smoothed her skirt. She moved away. Paris looked around the shop, running a hand over the dusty furniture. Five minutes went by.

There was a sound of footsteps and a man came in from the back of the store. He peered at Paris through a pair of heavy bifocals. He was an old man, stooped and gnarled. His skin was like the texture of old parchment and his hair was thick and white.

The girl came out of the shadows and spoke. "There's a man to see you, Mr. Shapp."

"Thank you, Judy," Shapp said. He peered at Paris again.

Paris said, "I'm from the State Police. Detective-Inspector Paris."

Paris was aware of a sound from the girl. She moved quickly behind an old counter and out of his vision.

"You're who?" Shapp asked.

"The State Police," Paris said. "Inspector Paris."

"Something is wrong, Inspector?"

"Yes," Paris said. "Mr. Shapp, you bought an old trunk at the Kolloway auction last Friday. Is that right?"

"Yes, I bought a trunk."

"What was in the trunk, Mr. Shapp?"

"You wait, Inspector," Shapp said. "I'll get a chair so you can sit down."

"I'll stand," Paris said. "What about the trunk, Mr. Shapp?"

"It was an old steamer trunk. Old, but serviceable."

"What was in it?"

"I have the trunk here. You can look at it. It's empty."

"It wasn't empty when you bought it, Mr. Shapp. What was in it then?"

"A few Japanese novelties. Why?"

"Were there any statues in there, Mr. Shapp?"

"Statues. Oh yes, little statues. On the shelf here. I didn't unpack the trunk, Inspector. Somebody else did." Shapp moved slowly across the room. "Here are the statues," he said, pointing. "Here. You can see they're cheap figurines, Inspector."

"You didn't find the statue of a horse, Mr. Shapp?"

"No, just these little things. I don't see so good. Is there a horse there?"

"No," Paris said. "This horse was larger. It was about twelve inches high."

"That's all I have, Inspector."

"Who was it that unpacked the trunk when it came in?"

Shapp hesitated. "Why are you asking, Inspector?"

"I wouldn't ask if I didn't have a reason, Mr. Shapp."

"That's a good answer," Shapp said, half-smiling. "It's a good answer, but it tells me nothing. Well, I have a partner. He unpacked the trunk."

"What's your partner's name?"

"Harold Dana."

"D-A-N-A?"

"Yes."

"Where is he now?"

"He isn't here."

"I know he isn't here," Paris said. "Where did he go?"

The girl moved into the light again. "He's away," she put in rapidly. "On a business trip. He's gone to Kansas City."

"How long ago?" Paris asked her.

"Three days ago," she said, breathing shallowly. "He won't be back for some time."

"And who are you?" Paris asked.

"Excuse me," Shapp said. "Maybe I should introduce you. This is Miss Judy Dana. Harold's sister."

"How do you do," Paris said to her, touching his hat. "Now, Miss Dana, how did your brother go to Kansas City?"

"He flew."

"What airline?"

"I don't know."

"What hotel is he staying at?"

"I don't know. He didn't tell us."

"Has he written or phoned?"

"No, not yet."

"How old is your brother, Miss Dana?"

"He's twenty-one," she said. "Why are you looking for him?"

"I didn't say I was looking for him, Miss Dana. I'm *asking* about him. What does he look like?"

"Oh, a nice young man," Shapp said. "Medium tall, good appearance. Light hair with a little red in it. Maybe a bit on the skinny side, but he'll fill out. He's a fine boy, Inspector."

"Isn't he a little young to be a partner, Mr. Shapp?"

"Why?" Shapp asked. "Does there have to be a special age?"

"No. But how long have you been in business together?"

"Six months."

"Where does he live?" Paris asked.

"In Eastern City," Shapp said.

"*Where* in Eastern City?" Paris asked patiently.

"With me," Judy Dana said quickly. "Out in Oakdale."

"What's the address?" Paris asked her.

"2245 Dudley Avenue."

"Do you have a picture of him, Miss Dana?"

"No," she said. "No picture."

"No? What about at the house?"

"No picture," she said.

"Where are your parents?" Paris asked.

Shapp said, "Their folks are dead, Inspector. Just the two children left, Harold and Judy. I knew their father. He was a fine man. What are these questions for, Inspector? What did Harold do wrong?"

Paris shook his head. "I want to know one thing more. Do you know a William Lakos?"

"The only Lakos I know is an art dealer."

"That's the one I'm talking about. Do you do business with him?"

"Never. I wouldn't do business with a man like that."

"What about Harold Dana? Does he know Lakos?"

"That I couldn't say, Inspector."

Paris looked at him, then across to the girl. Her eyes came up at him defiantly. "All right," Paris said slowly. "That's all for now, Mr. Shapp. But I'll want to see you again. Where will you be?"

"Where else could I be, Inspector?" Shapp said. "I'm here. I'm here all the time."

"And you, Miss Dana?"

"There's nothing you have to see me about," she said.

"There might be. Where can I get in touch with you?"

"You don't have to get in touch with me," she said coldly. "I don't like the way you act, and there's nothing I have to tell you."

"Don't fight," Shapp said to her gently. "The Inspector might have a reason." He turned to Paris. "You have her address, Inspector. You'll find her at home when you need her. Believe me, she won't run away from you."

Paris looked at her. The girl, her mouth taut, eyed him steadily.

"All right," Paris said abruptly. "Good-bye, Mr. Shapp."

He went to the door, opened it, the little bell jangling. Outside he turned right and walked the half-block to the corner.

8

THERE WAS A DRUGSTORE, ITS DOORS WIDE OPEN. PARIS went inside. In a telephone booth near the window, he dialed the operator.

"White Sands Beach," he said. "The Chief of Police."

He waited. The toll operator told him to deposit the coins. There was a buzz.

"White Sands Police," the voice said. "Chief Kay."

"Hello. This is Wade Paris."

"Hello," Kay said. "How are you doing up there, Inspector?"

"I've found a little," Paris said. "How are you doing down there?"

"I guess I ain't doing a thing," Kay said. "They've got my office here crowded with all kinds of experts, and the reporters are all over the Town Hall. The Commissioner's gone back to Capitol City and Coyne's going around looking very wise. The wiser he looks, I figure the less he knows. You want to talk to him?"

"Yes, Chief."

"He's probably outside getting his picture took. I'll call him."

Paris waited. Lieutenant Coyne came on the phone.

"You find something, Wade?" he asked.

"Yes," Paris said. "I've got a line on the baby-faced kid."

"That's fast work," Coyne said, elated. "I can use something right now. These reporters are like vultures."

"Let's make no mistake," Paris said. "This has to be kept quiet or we'll lose it. But here's the lead. You'd better get a man over to the Eastern City airport and check on a passenger named Harold Dana. D-A-N-A. Got it?"

"I've got it."

"The boy was supposed to have taken a flight to Kansas City last Sunday. I don't believe he did. But check their records. Check them back a week."

"I'll do that," Coyne said.

"All right," Paris said. "What have you found down there?"

"Nothing much," Coyne said. "A local fisherman went out in his charter boat with a passenger early this morning. His tender was just found up on the beach. Of course it might not mean a thing. It could have drifted loose while he was out there, and he might not have noticed it."

"What's the fisherman's name?" Paris asked.

"Carl Olsen."

"Is he still out to sea?"

"He's still out. I don't think it means anything. But I put in a call to the Coast Guard."

"All right," Paris said. "I'll keep in touch."

He hung up and went outside. There was a taxi stand on the corner with a single cab in it. The cab driver, sitting behind the wheel, was listening to the baseball game over his radio. Paris showed his shield. The man reached out and shut the radio off.

"I want you to tail me," Paris said. "Have you ever done it before?"

"No, sir."

"I'll tell you how," Paris said. "You can put on your meter, I'll pay for it. I'm going to follow somebody and I may have to do it on foot. If I do, you keep near me. Follow a half-block behind, not too obviously. Keep passing me and doubling back. But keep me in sight and in reach. If you see my arm go up, you'll know I need the cab then. You come in a hurry. Do you get it?"

"Yes, sir. I can do it."

"Good," Paris said. "I'll wait across the street where you can see me."

He crossed the intersection to the other side of the street. He stood close to the shaded side of a tenement building. He took out a cigarette. He smoked, his eyes on the antique shop. Ten minutes went by. He saw the flash of sun hit the opening door of the store.

Judy Dana came out, a black straw hat on her red hair, a black bag in her hand. Paris moved quickly around the corner. He edged back again. He saw her walking rapidly away from him along Somerset Street. He moved after her, keeping on the opposite side of the street, fifty feet behind, pedestrians between. The cab came by, passed him, and turned the corner sharply. Judy Dana stopped. She looked into a store window, then turned her head back. She started walking again, covering two blocks. The cab came by once more and stopped ahead.

Judy Dana turned left on Kingston Street and started up the hill. Paris, waiting at the corner, saw her look back. The cab came along, parked at the corner of Kingston and Somerset, motor purring gently.

Paris saw the girl enter a house halfway up the hill. He waited a moment. He ran up the street, along the tree-lined curb, feeling the steepness of the hill in his legs. The cab, gears clashing into action, passed him and took the turn at the intersection on top. Paris came by the building, slowed, noticing the door number 311, the ancient red-brick apartment house, the many-paned windows and the wrought-iron balcony along the second story. He came to the intersection and nodded his approval at the cab driver. He stood behind a lamp post at the corner and lit another cigarette.

The girl came out. She started down the street again, Paris waiting. She came to the corner of Somerset and stopped at the bus-stop marker. Paris turned and waved to the cab driver. The cab moved close to the curb. Paris got in.

"Drive down," he said. "She's waiting for a bus."

The cab inched down the street. The bus came along. Judy Dana got in. The bus moved away.

The cab turned right onto Somerset and followed, keeping behind, waiting at the intersections. The bus moved across the city to Central Square. Judy Dana stepped out, changed buses, getting into one marked DEPOT. The cab followed. The bus moved along Eastern Avenue and passed the wharves. It stopped at the railroad station. Judy Dana got out.

She went through the wide-arched entrance, the commuter crowd milling, flowing, criss-crossing. Paris was out of the cab, moving after her. He saw her cross the marble floor to the baggage room. He came to the newsstand. He stood behind it leafing a magazine. At the baggage-room counter Judy Dana was talking earnestly to the attendant. The attendant was shaking his head. She turned away, stood there indecisively, tapping her trim foot.

Now she left the counter. She went by the opposite side of the newsstand. Paris brought the magazine down as she went by. Her mouth was slightly parted, her eyes taut, looking straight ahead, not seeing. Paris let her go, watching her as she passed through the arched exit.

He went to the baggage room. The attendant was busy. Paris waited. The attendant turned around. Paris had his shield ready. The attendant looked at it and rubbed his hands nervously.

"That girl who was just here," Paris said. "What did she want?"

"What girl, sir?"

"That pretty redhead."

"That was some doll," the attendant said.

"Yes," Paris said. "What did she want?"

"She came here looking for a parcel. She didn't have the claim check."

"What was in the parcel?"

"She didn't tell me."

"What do you do in a case like that?"

"Well," the man said, scratching his head. "It all depends. She tells me her brother left a parcel here and he's lost the check. I ask her if it's a suitcase. She says no, it's a parcel, a box maybe. I tell her no checkee, no shirtee. Those are my orders. Then she wants to know if I remember her brother checking it. She tells me he's a tall, thin kid with reddish hair. And she tells me he's checked parcels here before. Imagine that? You know what I tell her?"

"No."

"I tell her we get hundreds of people here every day. I don't remember a tall, thin kid checking anything. Now I can remember a person if he really stands out. Say a guy's got a big birthmark on his face, or he's wearing spats, or he's got a cane or something. But he's got to be something out of the ordinary. Understand?"

"Yes," Paris said. "Have you seen this redheaded girl before?"

"No, sir." He winked at Paris. "Now she's different. Her I'd remember."

"What would you do if this girl came back and described the package? Would she get it then?"

"That's what she asked me. Well, in a case like that, if a person loses a check, they've got to describe the article. But they can't kid us about it. Anybody can describe a bag or a piece of luggage. They've got to tell us in detail what's *inside* the parcel. Then we take it upstairs to the station master and open it. If it's what they say it is inside, they sign for it and we give it to them. But this girl wouldn't even describe the outside of the package. So no dice. She ain't even sure her brother left the package here."

"Are there any names on these checks?" Paris asked.

"No names, sir. Just numbers."

"And do many people check items here? People who don't take trains?"

"Plenty." The man pointed to a card on the wall. "You see those rates? Fifteen cents a day. They're the cheapest rates in town. A lot of people know that. You take those lockers over there. You can only keep stuff in them twenty-four hours."

"Thanks," Paris said. "I want you to do something. If the girl comes back with the check, you grab it. Get a railroad cop and have her brought upstairs and hold her. Get the station master to call Captain Springer of the Eastern City Police. Have you got that?"

"Yes, sir."

"If a tall, redheaded kid shows up for a parcel, do the same thing. But watch yourself with him."

"Yes, sir," the man said. "Will do."

Paris left him. He went across the station and outside. The cab driver leaned excitedly from his window.

"The girl came out ten minutes ago," he called out. "She took an uptown bus."

"That's all right," Paris said. "You can drive me back to the cab stand."

9

IT WAS NOW TWO O'CLOCK IN THE AFTERNOON AND THE heat showed no signs of abating. Paris drove the State Police car up Kingston Street and parked in front of Number 311. He went up the ancient brick stairs and inside.

The hallway was clean, dark and deserted. The old brass letterboxes were highly polished. Paris peered at the little white name cards underneath. The small slot for Apartment Two was empty. Paris pressed the bell above it. He could hear it ringing from an apartment down the hall. He waited, rang again.

He went past the stairway, down the corridor to the door marked 2. He knocked. There was no answer.

He stepped away. He continued down the hall to the rear entrance. Out back in the sunlight, he looked up at the building. There were some sagging, rickety porches. Paris went around to the side. There was a man there, thin, undersized, with a sallow face, wearing a pair of faded coveralls. He was wheeling a galvanized barrel from a small wooden shed. Paris went up to him. The man set the barrel erect and straightened up. Paris showed his shield.

"You're the superintendent?" he asked.

"Yup," the man said. His armpits were wet with perspiration. He wiped his hands on the seat of his trousers.

"Who has Apartment Two?"

"That's Mr. Dana."

"Harold Dana?"

"Yup."

"His name isn't on the bell."

The man's forehead wrinkled. "It sure is. I've got all the names on. We've got no vacancies."

"His name isn't on the bell," Paris said.

The man's forehead wrinkled again. "That's sure funny. It was there an hour or so ago. I remember. I was polishing the brass."

"It's gone now," Paris said. "Somebody removed it. Where's Mr. Dana?"

"He ain't been around for a few days."

"You're sure?"

"He ain't here," the man said. "The gas meter man was around this morning. I let him into the apartment to read the meter. Mr. Dana isn't in there."

"Has anybody been around looking for him?"

"I seen his sister a couple of times. I don't know who else. I keep pretty busy, mister."

"How long has Mr. Dana lived here?"

"Three months."

"Alone?"

"Nobody else. He rented the apartment single."

"Thanks," Paris said. He left the man and went back inside the building. He went softly to the door marked 2 and put his ear flat against the panel. No sound.

He started to turn away, then stopped. He heard a slight rustle on the staircase above him. He pushed instinctively against the wall and moved toward the stairs.

There was a flash. The explosion roared out at him from above. The bullet screamed by his head, thudding into the woodwork.

Paris, his arm back, his service revolver out of his hip holster, crouched slightly. He edged along the wall toward the stairs. His eyes searched through the semi-darkness.

He heard footsteps clattering up the stairs away from him. He ran for the staircase. He went up them to the second-floor landing, his gun up, finger tensed on the trigger. He looked down the corridor, swung around the banister and continued up. Below he could hear doors opening, the shout of voices, a woman's panicky calling, a child whimpering. He came to the third floor, looked around. A door opened. A woman in a housedress peeked out, saw the gun, screamed and banged the door shut. There was the sound of a bolt sliding into place.

A noise above him, a sound of something slamming. He looked, saw the narrow stairway to the roof. Coming up fast, flattening to the side, he pushed against the roof door. It was locked. He ran back down the stairs again. The tenants were gathered in the halls now, babbling and running for their doors as they saw him coming. He ran down to the street. He went around his car and out to the middle of the road. His eyes searched the roof, then the rooftops of the adjoining buildings. He waited there, anxious, his gun down by his side.

The sound of a siren. A white-and-black police car careened around the corner of Somerset. It came up the hill and stopped in the middle of the street. Two cops came out, their service revolvers in their hands. They moved in on Paris warily.

Paris came to meet them, his leather folder out, flipping it impatiently. "You'd better take cover," he said to them. "It's somebody with a gun."

One of them holstered his revolver and ran back to the car. He slid into the seat and spoke into the radio-telephone. The other cop, young, uncertain, holding his gun awkwardly and uneasily in his hand, looked at the State Police car and then at Paris. He wet his lips.

"You'd better get out back," Paris said to him, pointing to the building. "Watch the alley."

The cop ran into the building, bumping into tenants now coming out into the street.

Sirens keened in the distance. A police car came around the top of the street and stopped there. Another police car turned the corner from Somerset, stopping and blocking the intersection. A fat policeman, dwarfed in the distance, came out of it with a riot gun in his hands. Paris scanned the rooftops, seeing nothing.

He put away his gun. He went into the building and down the hallway. He looked at the woodwork across from apartment 2.

The wood was splintered, the hole going deep. Paris took out a pencil and marked a circle around it.

A broad-shouldered young man came into the hallway, followed by a uniformed street sergeant. Paris turned around and looked at the young man tentatively.

"Hennessey?" Paris asked.

"Yes, sir," Hennessey said. "What happened, Inspector?"

"Somebody took a pot shot at me."

"In here?" Hennessey asked.

"From the staircase."

"You get a look at him, sir?"

"No," Paris said. "I don't know whether it was a him or a her. But whoever it was, got away through the roof."

"I've got the block covered," Hennessey said. He waited patiently, shifting his feet. "We'll have to have something to go on."

Paris shook his head. "You're right," he said. "There's nothing. The person could have pocketed the gun and mixed with the crowd. I guess we can call it off. Anyway, the bullet is in the wall here. I'll want it out."

Hennessey went over and looked at the wall. "Yes, sir," he said. "I'll call into headquarters."

"And I'll want to talk to Captain Springer," Paris said.

"You can use the telephone in my car," Hennessey said.

Paris went out. There was a detective car parked behind his. He went over and got inside. He lifted the phone. He spoke to the police dispatcher. He waited. Captain Springer came on the phone.

"Wade," Springer said, "what the hell's going on there at Kingston Street?"

"Somebody shot at me, Sam," Paris said. "He got away. You'll need some lab men here. I'd like to get a test of the bullet. It's in the wall."

"I'll send a crew out right away," Springer said. "You all right?"

"I'm fine," Paris said.

"What are you messing around with?"

"It's the Endicott case," Paris said.

"The Endicott case? I thought Coyne, the fair-haired boy, was running it. What is this anyway, Wade? You working under Coyne?"

"Around him," Paris said.

"Don't let me cuss over the phone," Springer said. "But I'm glad you're in on it, Wade. Dan Hallmark and me were old friends."

"I know," Paris said.

"Besides, Chief Koster wants us to get a line on it. Those Endicotts are Eastern City people. I've got Conlon and Rosen down at White Sands now. They're complaining Coyne's shutting them out. Who does he think he is? God?"

"I'd like to meet you later," Paris said.

"Don't shut me off," Springer said. "When?"

"I'll call you."

"Not too late," Springer said. "I'm not like you, Wade. I don't work twenty-four hours. I've got a home life too."

"I'll call you, Sam," Paris said.

He hung up, stepped out of the car. He went inside the building and spoke to Hennessey. When he came out, he got into his car and drove down to Post Office Square.

10

IT WAS A SHABBY BUILDING ON A SHABBY STREET ON THE fringe of the business district. The building was three stories high and carried no elevator. Paris walked up the stairs to the second floor. He passed offices marked taxidermist and mechanical dentist. The third office door was dusty and grimy. The black print said, WILLIAM LAKOS, ANTIQUES. Paris tried the knob. It was locked. He rapped twice. There was no answer. He bent down to the keyhole, his eyes peering in, spotting the edge of a flat-topped desk, a rumple of papers on it; a piece of faded rug and part of a chair.

He turned away and went down the stairs. In the first floor corridor, a colored janitor in a black cap was pushing a long-handled broom.

"Is Mr. Lakos around?" Paris asked him.

The man leaned on his broom and shook his head. "No. I ain't seen him since Saturday morning."

"Does he go away like that often?"

"Oh, sure. Sometimes he's gone for a week. This time I know he ain't been in since Saturday."

"Do you have his home address?" Paris asked.

"Now I don't know about that," the man said. "Mr. Lakos don't want us giving out his home address. He's touchy about those things. He don't even have the cleaning woman in his office. Cleans it himself."

Paris took out his folder and showed it. "It's important," he said. "What's Mr. Lakos' home address?"

The man looked down at the shield. His eyes came up and he smiled. "Now that's different, Inspector. He lives over in Mirror Park. Way out. 4320 Cheney Avenue."

"Thanks," Paris said. "Do you know if he has a telephone there?"

"I guess not, Inspector. If he has, it ain't listed."

"Is he married?"

The janitor shook his head. "I guess not. I never heard him speak of it."

"Does he have any employees?"

"No. He works by himself."

"You ever see a redheaded boy come up to visit him? A fellow about twenty-one years of age?"

"No, I can't say I have."

"You're sure?"

"I'm sure, Inspector."

"Thanks," Paris said. He went out of there, out to the street and into his car.

He drove the State Police car over the Matasset River and through Mirror Park. The time was now almost four-thirty, and the sun, lower in the sky, blazed in through the windshield. He passed the Mirror Park shopping center and squeezed the car through the traffic to Cheney Avenue. The houses, clustered at first, began to thin out. He passed the Mirror Park golf course, noticing the dry, brown fairways, the tree branches hanging lifelessly. Now there were mailboxes on posts along the road. The houses were more scattered.

4320 Cheney Avenue was a small, gray clapboard bungalow with a low, pitched roof. It was five hundred yards away from the nearest house. Across from it was the railroad embankment, and the straight lines of the telephone wires.

Paris drove up in front of the bungalow and parked on the gravel shoulder of the road. The rural letterbox was marked *Lakos* and the mail flag was down.

Paris walked across the gravel and up the cement walk to the front porch. On the floor boards were two bottles of milk and two rolled newspapers.

Paris pushed at the bell button. He heard it ring inside. He waited. He bent down and picked up one of the milk bottles. He looked at it. The milk was soured.

He went down the stairs and crossed the weed-tangled lawn to the pebbled driveway. He walked down to the small, one-car garage. The broad, beamed door had a fastened padlock. He went around to the side of the garage. There was a small, cracked window repaired with adhesive tape. Paris looked in.

There was a small, blue sedan inside. A tire tube lay in the corner. There were an oil can, a broken sawhorse and some rusted garden tools. Paris tried the window. It was locked.

He turned away. He went into the back yard, walking around a pile of rubbish. He went up the worn stairs to the rear door. He tried the knob. It was locked. Beside it was a window. The stained shade was fully drawn. He tried that. It was locked. He went down the stairs again. He stood in the yard, his face turned toward a house in the distance.

He went back up the rear stairs again. He looked in through the keyhole, seeing nothing. He put his nose there and sniffed. His nostrils tightened.

Suddenly he straightened up. He stepped back, then crashed the door with his shoulder. The door splintered at the lock, gave, and sprung open. Paris stumbled in.

It was a small entry and beyond it was a half-opened door. Paris opened it wider, holding his breath. He took out his handkerchief and put it to his nose.

He was in a small kitchen. He went quickly by a cheap, shoddy dinette set and unfastened the window. He opened it wide, tearing away the shade. His handkerchief still to his nose, he went across the broken, worn linoleum and into the dining room. There was a veneered-walnut set and buffet. He went through and into the living room.

The body lay face down on the floor, near the broken-springed sofa. One hand was out and crooked into a talon claw. The body was slightly bloated, a medium-sized man in a gray suit. The hair was black and awry. Under the body there was a large, dark stain that had spread out and dried on the bare floor. The back of the coat jacket was black, discolored and pulpy, and covered with flies. Paris waved them away with his free hand. They rose, large and fat, buzzed around, and began to settle down again.

Paris went out the way he had come, closing the door behind him. He stood in the hot sunlight, taking large draughts of air. He went down the stairs and around to the front of the house.

11

THE UNIFORMED MEN OVERFLOWED ONTO THE FRONT porch, waiting impatiently, hot and irritable. The basket had come two hours past and the body had gone out in it.

Captain Sam Springer of the Homicide Bureau came out onto the porch and took his hat off. His shock of white hair was damp. He took out a paper tissue and mopped his wet face. His tall, spare frame was slightly drooped, his collar unfastened and his tie unknotted.

He went over to Paris who was standing at the paint-faded railing. "That wraps it up for now," he said to Paris. "I'll get everybody out of here."

The men left now, clumping down the stairs. The conversations died away, cars geared into motion. A police photographer took a last flashlight picture of the house, got into a waiting car and moved away. A motorcycle cop waved the traffic by and started up his vehicle.

Paris was alone with Captain Springer. Springer stood there, rubbing his big, red-veined nose reflectively, looking across to the railroad tracks, his wise old face tired.

"I didn't want this damn job," Springer said. "I'm not as spry as I used to be, Wade."

"Next thing you'll be telling me," Paris said, "is that you were happy over there at the Cedar Heights precinct."

"Sure I was," Springer said. "I'm long past retirement. I wanted to quit. But what happened? Koster put me upstairs in Homicide." He turned and looked at Paris. "You smirking at me, Wade?"

"You could have refused it." Paris grinned. "I was thinking of the times we've worked together. Always the same complaint, old age. But you'll never quit. You're an old fire horse."

"That's what you think," Springer said. He took out a small, black briar pipe and fumbled for his pouch. He filled the pipe slowly, tamping in the tobacco with an experienced finger. "Old fire horses drop dead too. Where do *you* get all the energy, Wade? I know you're young, but a man's got a limit."

"I've got a job to do," Paris said.

"Sure, but you don't have to punch a time clock. What do you think Coyne's doing down there at White Sands? I'll bet he's behind the Chief's desk issuing orders like everything and slopping up pitchers of beer."

Paris said nothing. Springer shook his head slowly. "I'm sorry, Wade," he said. "You're thinking of Dan Hallmark, and that's all that counts with you. I got tied up with Dan on a killing once. He was grooming you then. He said you were as stubborn as a mule and you had all the fervor of a knight looking for the Holy Grail. I don't know if it's so good being an idealist. You came up fast, I'll grant that. But you've gone as far as you can go. From now on it's knowing the right people. I don't think you'd go along with those people, Wade."

"I don't deceive myself," Paris said.

"Okay," Springer said. "So you won't. So you'll be shuffled out some day. And maybe you'll have the satisfaction of doing your job the best you could. It's nice to have satisfaction like that, but it don't pay off in groceries."

"I notice *you* never ran with the crowd," Paris said. "They say you could have made Deputy Superintendent, maybe Chief."

"Well, I'm a renegade. I'm old and crotchety. Besides I earn enough for Emma and me. The kids are all grown up and married and the grandchildren, God bless them, don't ask for much. But you're the new crop, Wade. College, the FBI Academy. Science and lab work. And does it do any good? You're still on Civil Service pay, and you've still got hack ward heelers like your commissioner to kowtow to. People don't have much use for cops and most of the time I don't blame them. We don't attract the right class of people to the job."

"I'll admit that," Paris said.

"It's the country we live in," Springer said. "It's a lawless country. I guess we've got a higher percentage of crime than any country in the world. People expect you to take a buck. They do it in private industry. You tell me one decent, upright citizen who hasn't called up a politician to get a tag fixed. They say if you're smart, you'll take. If you don't take, then you're stupid. What chance has a cop got? You can't have crooked people and straight cops. People don't think it's a disgrace doing it. The disgrace is getting caught."

"Maybe you have a solution," Paris said.

Springer puffed slowly at his pipe. "Maybe I have, son. Cops are pressured from top and bottom, from politicians to racketeers. But no racketeer can stay in business without connections. Take your politician. He's a man in public office and he's got a responsibility. He handles public safety and public funds. So if he runs for public office, he should take a stiff qualifying exam before he's eligible. That would eliminate some of the ignorant stump-hollerers with the sticky fingers. The ones who are all noise and no brains. And if you'll pay them well, all along the line, you'll find it cheaper on the tax rate. You'll have superior men and less padding. It works with these towns that have city managers. It'll work with cops too."

"It's an idea," Paris said.

"I get philosophical in my old age," Springer said. "And I talk and talk. But right now we've got Lakos on our hands." He took the pipe out of his mouth, looked at the bowl, and knocked it against the porch railing. "Well, what have we got? The M. E. tells us Lakos had been dead three days, maybe less. He can't figure it exactly on account of the warm weather. He had two slugs through the stomach and there's nary a fingerprint around."

"You didn't expect it to be easy, did you?"

"Hell, no." Springer said. "Since when did you make them easy for me? I remember this Lakos. We had him in once or twice. He was a soft one. He talked easy. That's what somebody figured here. They didn't want him to talk. It's going to be hard to get a line on Lakos. He lived small. Nobody worked for him. He had no family. He was a small-time chiseler with a small-time record. Maybe if he'd have gotten bigger he wouldn't have died that way. The bigger they get, the more natural they die. You ever study that, Wade?"

"Yes," Paris said. "Well, I think we can pin the Lakos killing at some time Monday. He used his milk Monday morning, but not from then on. And it ties in with the Endicott case. He was killed with a power gun."

"I'll go along with that," Springer said. "The gun fired at you in the hallway was a power weapon. Those slugs match up, Wade."

"Yes," Paris said. "And they'll match up with the slugs at White Sands Beach. They're from the .357 Magnum. But where's the rest of it?"

"Well," Springer said, rubbing his nose. "There's no Chinese statue on Lakos' mantel, if that's what you want. You've got to find this Dana kid. I'm for sending out an eight-state dodger on him."

"We'll do that," Paris said. "I'll try to get a picture of him. What about your crew at Lakos' office?"

"Nothing so far," Springer said. "They're still working there. We'll have to wait until they report in."

"Then I'll go back to your office and wait. I've got some calls to make anyway."

Springer looked across the broad fields at the red setting sun. "It's half-past seven," he said. "I've had no dinner. My wife is going to keep it in the oven until it's all dried up. You know how often that happens, Wade?"

"I know," Paris said. "You could have become a streetcar conductor with regular hours. You go ahead home, Sam. You can come downtown after dinner."

"Come on home with me," Springer said. "You look peaked."

"No, thanks," Paris said. "But I would like to have this house covered."

"I've got it spotted from a place up the road," Springer said. "Personally I don't think anybody's coming back. The smell would drive them away."

It was a plain, bare office on the second floor of Police Head-quarters. The desk and chairs were of utility oak. The walls carried bulletin boards, a large, pin-pointed map of Eastern City, and a picture of the Police Pistol Team. There was an electric wall clock that said nine p.m.

Paris, behind the desk, rubbed his eyelids and snapped off the small fluorescent lamp. He pushed the papers aside and stood up. He flexed his legs, walked across the room and opened the frosted-glass door.

The big squad room was hot and stuffy, holding a half-dozen detectives in shirtsleeves. At a desk in a corner two of them were playing gin rummy. A fat, white-shirted detective, with a cigar in his mouth and a gun in a black-leather shoulder holster, left the teletype machine and went to his desk. Paris crossed the room to him.

"Anything come in yet from Lakos' office?" Paris asked.

"Nothing, Inspector," the man said. "They've got a safe there that they've got to drill open." He shifted the cigar in his mouth. "They tell me it's a damn good safe for such a crummy joint. They've called another man in."

The loud speaker in the room signaled, then spoke. The men in the back of the room looked up briefly. *Car 22. Car 22. Disturbance 751 Pine Street. 751 Pine Street. Car 22.* The loud-speaker clicked off. The men went back to their game. Near the door a uniformed man worked at his typewriter, his face sallow in the light of the lamp.

The outer door opened and Captain Springer walked in. He went over to the teletype machine and read it. "You seen this stuff, Inspector?" he called to Paris.

"Yes," Paris said. He followed Springer into the private office and closed the door.

"I called the Newgate Barracks," Paris said. "They're bringing in the Endicott slugs to match up."

"They'll match," Springer said, taking off his hat. He went over and turned on the electric fan. "It ain't cooled off any. What else?"

"They checked at the airport," Paris said. "Nobody by the name of Harold Dana took a plane. They checked back a week."

"Well, you figured that, Wade," Springer said, sitting down.

"Yes," Paris said. "But now there's something else. I've got a report from White Sands on that fisherman, Carl Olsen. The Coast Guard found his fishing boat late this afternoon. It was drifting three miles off Saint Anne's Light. Empty."

Springer leaned forward on his elbows, his face serious. "That's not good," he said. "We're up against somebody real smart. And this person ain't one damn bit afraid of cops either."

"No," Paris said. "That's the trouble, Sam. Things are happening all around me and I can't stop them."

Springer picked up a pencil and made a doodle on a sheet of paper. "You can't do everything yourself," he said. "You'd better let me bring in this Shapp and the Dana girl. I'll shake them."

"It's too soon," Paris said. "But you can set it up, Sam. You can stake out Shapp's store and Miss Dana's house."

"I'm way ahead of you," Springer said, "I did that this afternoon." He stood up and went over to the wall map. "And we're watching Kingston Street and the Lakos house. I've got men at Lakos' office. I don't think this killer is coming back."

"I think he did come back," Paris said. "I think he came back to White Sands Beach with all those cops around."

"He came back *there* all right," Springer said thoughtfully. "And he could still be there too."

"I hate to think so," Paris said. "But that's the possibility. You'd better get me a search warrant for Harold Dana's apartment. We'll look there in the morning."

"What do you need a warrant for? You going to be legal about it?"

"Yes."

"All right. But you ought to get some rest now, Wade."

"No. I'm going over to see Judy Dana first. I think we'll have to hold her. It might flush her brother out."

"That's sensible," Springer said. "What about the old man?"

"You mean Shapp?"

"Yes."

"Whatever he's doing," Paris said, "I don't think he's doing for himself. He's covering for Dana. We'll watch the old man. I don't think he'll go anywhere."

"You don't want to sweat him?"

"Not tonight. We can do that in the morning."

"You want somebody to go with you to Miss Dana's?"

"I don't need anybody. You've got a man outside."

"But not inside. That's the trouble with you, Wade. Some day you'll be looking for help. What if the girl's brother is there? He's been shooting good."

"He won't be around," Paris said. "If I thought so I wouldn't go alone. I'm not that much of a hero, Sam."

"I don't know about that," Springer said. "I've seen you do things before."

Paris tapped him on the shoulder, picked up his hat and opened the door. The loudspeaker droned something as he crossed the outer room. He opened the outer door and went into the corridor. He went down the stairs and outside to the car. He swung it around and drove out to Oakdale.

12

2245 DUDLEY AVENUE WAS AN OLD WHITE HOUSE WITH AN old-fashioned turret, a cupola, and a gambrel roof. Paris, stopping at the curb, saw a nondescript sedan down the street. The sedan had a police shortwave antenna behind it.

There was a light in the living room. Paris left the car and went up the stairs to the small veranda. He rang the bell.

Judy Dana answered the door. She was wearing a short-sleeved blue jersey and white shorts that fitted tightly around her shapely thighs. On her feet were a pair of brown-leather moccasins with fringed flaps.

"Hello," Paris said, taking off his hat. "You look cool and comfortable. You staying home tonight?"

"Yes," she said.

"May I come in?"

"No," she said. She started to close the door.

Paris held it open with his arm. "It's better I come in," he said. "Otherwise I'll have to talk to you at Police Headquarters."

She stared at him, eyes unwavering. Suddenly she swung the door aside so hard that the glass rattled. Paris went in. He followed her into the living room.

The room was high-ceilinged, old and ornate. There were huge, dark pieces of carved mahogany, mohair chairs with tasseled antimacassars. A large grand piano stood in a corner, draped with a fringed shawl. There were velvet drapes at the windows. On the dark wood tables were many bottles and jars made of Sandwich glass. Paris went over and picked up a small-necked, lacy-patterned vase.

"An antique," he said to her. "Do you go in for antiques, Miss Dana?"

"They belonged to my father. My father was a collector. He didn't have enough money to go into it much."

"Do you like antiques too, Miss Dana?"

"Yes," she said curtly. "My brother and I inherited my father's love for them."

"Where is your brother now, Miss Dana?"

"I told you once. He flew to Kansas City."

"No," Paris said. "That's a silly lie. He didn't go to Kansas City."

Paris watched her, waiting for an answer. Her face reddened, but she didn't speak. Paris sat down in a chair.

There was a clumping sound in the hallway. Paris looked toward the doorway, half-rising from his chair. An old woman came into the room. She was bent and white-haired, and she hobbled with a cane. One leg was encased in a large black boot with a high platform. She wore a long, dark, ankle-length dress. There was a high collar around her withered neck.

Paris stood up. Judy said, "This is my aunt, Mrs. Pettigrew. She lives here with me. She doesn't hear very well." She raised her voice. "Auntie," she said loudly, "this is *Mr.* Paris."

Mrs. Pettigrew bobbed her head. "Good evening," she said. Her voice was metallic, tone-flat. "Warm, isn't it? Very warm. Judy, offer your young man some lemonade."

"He doesn't want any," Judy Dana said. "He'll be leaving soon."

"Nonsense," Mrs. Pettigrew said. "He'll want lemonade."

"No, thank you," Paris said.

Mrs. Pettigrew half-smiled. "There, Judy. The young man said he likes lemonade. It only takes a minute. And I won't stay here and gossip. I came to tell you I'm going upstairs to my room. I'll say good night."

"Good night," Paris said.

Mrs. Pettigrew bobbed her head again. Judy Dana said, "Please excuse me. I'll have to go with her and get her ready for bed."

They went out. Paris went over to the piano and looked at two framed pictures there. One was of a middle-aged, light-haired man with a small mustache. Beside it was the picture of a pretty, matronly woman. There was a small table with another picture on it. Paris went over and looked at it. It was a photograph of a young girl in dancing costume and ballet slippers. There was no picture of Harold Dana. Paris sat down. He took out his cigarettes and lit up. Judy Dana came back into the room.

Paris said, "Do you have a job, Miss Dana?"

She sat down across from him. "Yes," she said.

"What kind of work do you do?"

"I'm a secretary. I work at the Oakdale branch of Eastern City Gas and Light."

"How long?"

"Two years. Since getting out of secretarial school."

Paris looked at the end of his cigarette, at the long ash. Judy Dana stood up. She brought over an amber-colored ashtray. She sat down again.

Paris said, "Do you know a man named Walter Almieda?"

"No," she said.

"He's an artist."

"I don't know any artists, Inspector."

"Do you know a Mr. Noble?"

"No."

"A Mr. Hanft?"

"No."

Paris puffed at his cigarette. "Do you know a William Lakos?"

Her face turned away quickly, her hands straightening the doily on the arm of her chair. "No," she said.

"Did you know Charles Endicott?"

"No."

"He was murdered last Monday night."

"I read the papers," she said tersely.

"Did your brother Harold know him?"

"No," she said.

"Do you know anything about an antique Chinese horse, Miss Dana?"

"I don't know any horses, of any kind."

"Does your brother?"

"No," she said. She trembled, rubbed her hands briskly on her arms.

"Why are you shivering, Miss Dana?"

"I'm cold."

Paris inhaled the smoke slowly. "What are you so frightened about?"

"I'm not frightened."

"You are," Paris said. "You've been putting on an act. You've been trying to show a temper you don't have. And you've been lying."

She stood up. "Is that all you have to say, Inspector?"

"No," he said. "There's no sense lying, Miss Dana. Nor was there any sense in removing your brother's name from the bell at Kingston Street."

"I don't know what you're talking about," she said.

"All right, let's stop this jockeying around," Paris said. "Your brother doesn't live here with you, Miss Dana. Also, he knew William Lakos. He knew Charles Endicott. He didn't go to Kansas City. He's been trying to peddle a Chinese horse. How many lies does that make, Miss Dana?"

"Please," she said. "I'm upset tonight. Please go."

"If I go now, I take you with me. I'll hold you on suspicion as an accessory. And you'll stay in jail until we find your brother. You're a poor liar, Miss Dana. I think you'd better tell me the truth."

"I'd rather go to jail," she said.

"Don't talk like a martyr," he said. "You're not being noble, you're being foolish. You're not protecting your brother this way. You're harming him. He's tangled up with a Chinese horse. There have been three murders because of it, and possibly a fourth. Whatever his connection is, rightly or wrongly, his life isn't worth a nickel. And you're making it worse by lying." He put the cigarette into the ashtray and mashed it. He looked at her. Her head was down. The room was quiet.

"All right," Paris said. "We'll send out an alarm. We'll go after him. And it can end up with some trigger-happy cop shooting him down and killing him. I've seen that happen more than once too. And another thing, if he isn't the man we want, then somebody else is looking for him too. And that person has a gun and has been using it. And he'll use it on your brother."

Her head came up. Her eyes were wet. "My brother did nothing wrong," she said.

"Then why is he hiding?"

"I don't know," she said. She came over and sat down beside him. "Please. Don't you think I want to find him? I've been desperate. I've looked everywhere for him. I don't know what to do next."

"And you don't know how he got into this thing?"

She shook her head. "No."

"Yes, you do," Paris said. "You know he and Mr. Shapp bought an old trunk at the Kolloway auction. While your brother was unpacking it, he found something wrapped in old newspapers or hidden away in the bottom of the trunk. It was a T'ang horse. I don't know if your brother knew it was valuable then. He may have found out by trying to sell it to William Lakos. Anyway, he didn't sell it. He went to Sunset Point and tried to sell it to Mr. Endicott. Endicott wanted to examine it. Your brother wouldn't wait, or couldn't wait. He brought the horse back to Eastern City. He put it in the baggage room at the railroad station. Now he's hidden out somewhere. Is that right so far, Miss Dana?"

"I don't know," she said. "Honestly, I don't. I'm all confused."

"You weren't confused when you went to the baggage room," Paris said. "How did you know the horse was there?"

"I didn't know. I *thought* it was there. But I wasn't sure. All I knew was that Harold had checked things there before."

"What reason would he have for checking things before?"

"He had reasons."

"All right. How did you know about the horse?"

"Because Mr. Shapp told me. Then after Harold disappeared I kept going to his apartment. He wasn't there. I went to the baggage room as a last resort. Maybe, maybe he came back after the horse. In that way I'd know he was still in the city. But he didn't show up at the baggage room either. Or if he did, the man couldn't remember anyway. But I had no other way of looking for him."

"And how long has Harold been missing?"

"Almost a week now. Since last Friday."

"And why didn't you go to the police?"

"I waited. I thought he would come back."

"No," Paris said. "You knew he had done something wrong. That was the reason. He had been working with William Lakos."

"No," she said.

"It's not plausible," Paris said. "You're lying again."

"No," she said.

A telephone rang somewhere. She jumped up and ran into the hall. Paris heard her speak. She came back.

"It's for you," she said dully.

Paris went into the hallway and picked up the phone. "Hello," he said.

"How you doing?" Captain Springer asked.

"Not good," Paris said.

"Well, we found something," Springer said. "We got Lakos' office safe opened. There was some junk in it. A couple of little statues, some dishes and other things. He was foxy all right. There was thirty-five thousand dollars in cash in there too. What do you think of that?"

"What's so surprising?" Paris asked.

"What's so surprising? Why, we had him in on small charges a half-dozen times. He never posted bond himself. He always used a professional bondsman, screaming all the time how poor he was. Well, it serves him right. He lived mean and small. A guy like that would never have spent it anyway."

"You said something about statues. Did you find the horse there?"

"No, these were little statues, about six inches high. But there was something else, Wade. A receipt signed by Harold Dana. Lakos paid him two hundred and fifty dollars for a horse statue. The receipt said he'd get two-fifty more when Lakos sold the horse. But I don't see no horse."

"What was the date of the note?"

"The twentieth of July. That was last Friday. How does it sound to you, Wade?"

Paris looked over toward the living room. "Not good," he

said. "I didn't expect it. I think we'd better go over and see Mr. Shapp now."

"Now? You know what time it is?"

"I know."

"Well, there's no sense arguing with you," Springer said. "I'll meet you at Shapp's in a half-hour. You'd better crack this case, Wade. Else I'll never get no sleep."

"I'll see you," Paris said.

He hung up and went into the living room. Judy Dana looked at him anxiously.

"Maybe this will wake you up," Paris said to her. "Your brother sold the horse to William Lakos. Lakos was found murdered this afternoon. Did you know that, Miss Dana?"

"I heard it on the radio," she said tonelessly.

"So you knew that," Paris said. "The horse is gone. It's not very good for your brother. Do you want to tell me anything now, Miss Dana?"

"Please," she said. "I've nothing to tell you. Nothing."

"All right," Paris said. "I'll let you sleep here tonight. Not because I have any sympathy for you, but because of your aunt. You'll have to make arrangements for her care."

"What are you going to do?"

"I'm taking you downtown tomorrow. In the meantime, you won't leave the house. If you do, you'll be picked up outside."

"No, you couldn't do that."

"Yes," Paris said. "I'm doing it."

13

IT WAS A TINY ONE-ROOM EFFICIENCY APARTMENT ABOVE the store. There were a pullman kitchenette and a bathroom. In the main room there were an old brass bed and two upholstered living-room chairs, a table and two wooden chairs, a high chest of drawers.

"I'll have to have the true story," Paris was saying to Shapp.

Captain Springer leaned back in his chair and puffed at his pipe. Mr. Shapp, in woolen robe and carpet slippers, stood up and shuffled over to the bed. He stroked a bed post.

"Solid brass, Inspector," he said. "My wife died in that bed. We had our own house then. I sold the house after. What does an old man like me need? The bed, that's all. Soon I'll die in that bed too."

Captain Springer put his pipe down. "Don't talk about dying," he said. "It makes me nervous at my age."

"I'll have to have the true story," Paris said again. "You keep changing the subject, Mr. Shapp."

"I'm an old man," Shapp said, smiling gently. "You must be patient with me."

"I'm arresting Miss Dana in the morning," Paris said. "I'm going to get the truth, one way or another."

Shapp blinked his eyes. "You're arresting Judy, Inspector? A young girl like her?"

"Yes."

"But how can you put a child like that in jail?"

"She's been obstructing justice," Paris said. "She's been acting as an accessory in a crime."

"Ah," Shapp said. "So serious you are. Too bad. And you're so young too, Inspector. I know how it is with the young. They have a duty to perform, and nothing must stand in their way. Their hearts mustn't feel anything. You think you're fooling me?" He raised his hand and shook his head. "No, don't stop me. I know, I know. I've watched you. Your heart goes out to that girl. I could see it when you were in the store this morning. And who would blame you? She's such a warm, beautiful girl. But you don't allow yourself to think of it."

"This doesn't buy you a thing, Mr. Shapp," Paris said.

"There's no girl like Judy," Shapp said doggedly. "She's one in a million. She has love for her brother. She *would* go to jail to protect him."

"Then that's where she's going," Springer said.

"No," Shapp said. "She mustn't go to jail. That would be evil." He sighed and sat down slowly. "All right, if Judy won't tell you, I will have to do it. I'll tell you everything. I know the family, the aunt, Mrs. Pettigrew. I knew Judy's father, Jonathan Dana. Fine man, the father. He used to buy a little glass from me once in a while. He never had a lot of money, but a good, straightforward man he was. He died two years ago. He left seven thousand dollars. Judy came to me six months ago and she talked to me about a partnership for her brother. She had the seven thousand dollars. I need help here, so I say yes." He smiled softly. "Well, maybe I don't need the help, but I say yes anyway. Hal came into business with me. A nice young boy."

"What did Miss Dana get out of it?" Paris asked.

"What could she get? Nothing. She told me she had to take care of her brother. He needed the money more than her. That's the kind of girl Judy is. The boy is a good boy. I feel toward him like I would feel toward a grandson. I never had no children, Inspector."

"I appreciate all that," Paris said. "But I'm talking about a trunk."

Shapp nodded his head vigorously. "I'll talk about the trunk too," he said. "The girl don't have to go to jail for it. I bought the trunk at an auction. Harold was with me. We brought it back here. What was in the trunk, I'm not sure. I saw some cheap bric-a-brac in there but it was only a quick look. I went upstairs for a few minutes, and I left Harold to unpack the trunk. When I came down, Harold was gone. The door to the store was locked. I didn't see him since. That's the story."

"But not the entire story," Paris persisted. "You're keeping something back."

"You're a good policeman," Shapp said. "Yes, I've been keeping it back. It's hard for me to say it. But I don't want Judy to be blamed too. Harold was stealing things from the store."

"Yes," Paris said. "He was taking them to Lakos."

"Mind you, it was nothing," Shapp said. "Only little things. I don't keep an inventory." He tapped a temple with a misshapen finger. "Here is my inventory. In my head. I'm here in business a long time. Over fifty years. So if one thing isn't in its accustomed place, I know."

"You did nothing about this stealing?" Springer asked.

"What am I going to do, Captain?" Shapp asked. "The boy is young. It's a bit of foolishness and I know he'll get over it. He likes to go to the dog track at night. So maybe when the dog track closes in the fall, Harold will stop taking things."

Paris said, "And Miss Dana didn't know about this?"

"No. I would never tell her."

"But she found out. How?"

"It's true there is a Chinese horse," Shapp said. "Harold picked it up somewhere. You say it came from the trunk, Inspector. Judy and I didn't know that. We were afraid Harold stole it somewhere else. We knew he took this Chinese horse to William Lakos. Lakos gave him two hundred and fifty dollars for it. He told Harold he would give him another two-fifty if he sold the horse. Lakos said he was taking a chance because maybe the horse wasn't worth anything."

"How do you know all this?" Springer asked.

"Because," Shapp said, "Lakos came here Saturday, the day after Harold disappeared. He told me about it. He showed me the note. He said Harold took the horse away and he wanted it back. To him it was a legal sale. Then I found out about the other things. Harold was taking stuff from the store and putting them in the baggage room of the railroad station. He would keep them there until Lakos would come to the station and close the deals with him."

"And Miss Dana found that out too?" Paris asked.

"She was in the store looking for her brother when Lakos came. Lakos wasn't ashamed to tell her. It made Judy very upset. She was afraid for her brother, Inspector. She didn't want him to go to jail for stealing. And she's worried sick wondering where he is now."

"Had she been to Harold's apartment?" Springer asked.

"Yes. Five or six times. Harold never came back."

"And you have no idea where he is?" Paris asked.

"No," Shapp said. "I don't even know where to look."

"Well," Springer said, tapping the pipe stem against his teeth, "we'll look for him. But we're going to need a picture."

"I have a picture," Shapp said. He turned to look at Paris. "Judy isn't in trouble now?"

"Not at the moment," Paris said. "I'll know more when I check. It all depends on Captain Springer."

Springer hunched his shoulders. "I don't want her. She doesn't know anything. She got herself all fouled up running interference for her brother."

"What about this partnership?" Paris asked Shapp. "Is it an equal partnership?"

"Yes. Harold draws a salary. We figure the profits at the end of the year."

"Is it a corporation?"

"No. Why should I have a corporation?"

"I'm asking for this reason," Paris said. "According to the law, a partner can't steal from an unincorporated partnership. It would be like stealing from himself."

"I was just going to say that," Shapp said eagerly. "So Harold has done nothing wrong. I want to bring that out. If it's like you say, that the horse came from the trunk, then Harold didn't steal it."

"No," Paris said. "He didn't steal it."

"Then I must call Judy right away and tell her. Right away I'll call her. You don't know what this is going to mean to her."

"Wait a minute," Springer said, putting his pipe into his pocket. "There's one thing more. William Lakos is dead."

"Dead?" Shapp asked. "He was a young man. Why is he dead?"

"He was murdered two days ago," Springer said. "We found him this afternoon."

Shapp looked at him. His lower lip moved. He bowed forward in his chair. "That's very bad, Captain," he said. "Very, very bad."

"Yes," Paris said. "Then there's Charles Endicott and Lieutenant Hallmark. All murdered because of this Chinese horse. You see how important it is that we find Harold Dana."

Shapp's body rocked in the chair. "I see," he said tonelessly. "I was going to get you his picture, Inspector. But now maybe you'd better get it yourself. It's in the top drawer of the chiffonier."

Paris stood up and went over to the tall chest of drawers. He opened the top one. The picture was in there, a small three-by-five snapshot. He looked at it. The face was thin, young and immature. The features were good-looking, resembling Judy Dana's.

"His hair is on the reddish side," Shapp said. "It don't show in the picture."

"We'll make a note of that," Paris said. He passed the photo to Springer. "What do you figure his weight at, Sam?"

"Well," Springer said, rubbing his nose. "What did you say his height was?"

"About five-ten," Paris said.

"I'd give him about a hundred and thirty pounds," Springer said.

"Yes," Shapp said, nodding his head. "He's kind of skinny."

"We'll keep in touch with you," Paris said to him. "Thanks for the co-operation."

"You please find that boy," Shapp said. "I don't care about no horse. And when you find him, treat him nice. Please understand. I need him here. I want him here."

"We understand," Paris said.

They went out. They walked down the stairs and through the back entrance. When they came around to the front of the store, Springer stood in front of his black headquarters car for a moment. His face was solemn and thoughtful. He lifted his arm and looked at his strap watch under the light of the street lamp.

"After twelve," he said. "I'll go over to the office and have the picture printed. We'll also include the car registration. Then I'm going home."

"Yes," Paris said. "I think we can call it quits for tonight. Will you have that search warrant in the morning?"

"I'll have it when I pick you up," he said. "Good night, Wade."

"Good night," Paris said.

He waited until Springer got into his car, turned the lights on and drove away. Paris crossed the street and got into the State Police car. He started it up and moved away slowly. When he came by the cab stand on the corner, he saw a plainclothes man in a doorway. The man waved his hand in a short arc. Paris waved back. He passed by, and drove downtown to the Eastern Plaza Hotel.

In his room, with windows wide-open, Paris unhooked his holster and removed his revolver. He took out his cleaning kit and ran the small ramrod through the barrel. He reamed the chamber and oiled it. He put the gun back into the holster and rubbed his red-rimmed eyes.

He pulled his shirt off. He went to the bed and pulled the covers back. The telephone on the bedside table rang sharply. Paris went over and picked it up.

"White Sands Beach calling," the operator said. "Is this Detective-Inspector Paris?"

"Yes," Paris said.

"One moment, please."

Paris waited. There was a click, and Lieutenant Coyne's voice came on.

"Wade?" he asked.

"Yes," Paris said.

"I'm in trouble down here," Coyne said. "You'd better come down here right away."

Paris rubbed his aching eyes again. He said, "What's up?"

"The fisherman," Coyne said. "Carl Olsen. His body was washed up on the beach a half-hour ago."

14

IT WAS TWENTY MINUTES PAST TWO IN THE MORNING. The sky was dark, deep, star-studded. The tide was at its height, swishing in and bubbling onto the sand in a white phosphorescent sud. On the beach, the White Sands volunteer fire engine, hub deep in the sand, had its floodlight along the shore. At the far end of the beach two State Police cars, their spotlights blazing, moved long probing white fingers across the water. Along the edge of the water, a half-dozen troopers splashed, their boots calf-deep, flashlights winking.

Against the sea wall, people stood watching. Matches flared up and died away as cigarettes were lighted. The people, talking in whispers, edged away as Paris pushed through. He walked along the sand. He looked across the water at Sunset Point. The white Endicott house, in the light of the waning moon, stood alone, dark, bleak, and lifeless.

Standing in front of the fire truck was Colonel Davies, supervisor of state detectives. The Colonel, straight, rigidly erect, his black Homburg hat set squarely on his head, was talking angrily to Lieutenant Coyne.

Paris stepped up and saluted. The Colonel saluted back, said, "Hello, Wade. I'm glad you're here." He turned to Coyne again and his fine white mustache quivered. "What are you looking for?" he asked. "How many more bodies do you expect to wash up?"

"It's not that," Coyne said sullenly. "I thought something else might come in. The weapon."

"The man's head was bashed in," Davies said. "A heavy-weighted instrument. It wouldn't come in with the tide."

"But there's always a hope," Coyne said.

"I didn't fly down from Capitol City to talk about hopes," Davies said. "I want action here and I want it fast. Now you stop this ridiculous exhibition of yours. Get those lights off, Coyne, and send these people home."

"But the Commissioner——" Coyne started to say.

"The Commissioner isn't here," Davies said crisply. "And as long as *I'm* here you're not going to put on a Broadway show. And I don't want an argument. Do you hear me, Coyne?"

"Yes, sir," Coyne said. He turned and stamped away through the sand. Davies watched him go.

"It's a disgrace," he said. "A damn disgrace. I've tried to build an organization. I wanted young blood, college blood, smart blood. I wanted an organization that was clean, alert and incorruptible. I got the Commonwealth to put in the best equipment money could buy. I organized a department of legal medicine and affiliated it with the best medical school in the state. Now I've got political nincompoops and nepotism to spoil it."

He stopped and watched the lights blink out, the darkness folding over them.

"Coyne's got no right in this job down here," Davies said. "His brother may be Lieutenant-Governor, but that doesn't wash with me. The Commissioner had no right to go over my head either. It's not good for discipline. But Coyne's not a bad cop in spite of it. I know that because we trained him."

"No, sir," Paris said. "He's a pretty good cop."

"Sure he is," Davies said. "Or I wouldn't have him. But his experience has been mostly traffic safety, not homicides. I don't go for these ward-alderman shenanigans. This isn't a two-bit knifing in some beer joint. An Endicott has been killed. Also one of my own boys, Dan Hallmark. I don't like that at all, Wade."

"No, sir," Paris said.

"I know how you were with Dan Hallmark. Well, I feel the same way' about him. But it isn't Dan Hallmark any more. It's three men that have been murdered, one of them right under our nose. A fourth in Eastern City."

Paris said nothing.

"The Commissioner is a big, overgrown idiot," Davies said. "He's an exhibitionist and a sideshow barker. He's going to make himself famous and at the same time get himself in solid with the big boys. All right, let him try. So far all he's done is make a damn fool of himself."

"That doesn't help me any," Paris said.

"I know it doesn't," Davies said. "You're in the middle. Now you've done some good work in Eastern City. But while you were doing it, look what happened here. Coyne's got every state cop from miles around. Young cops, smart cops, with pretty uniforms and weapons. We don't even have a highway patrol in this sector, that's how many men we've thrown in here. And what happens? Right under their noses a fisherman gets murdered. I don't know what to say. We're a laughingstock. They'll say a troop of Boy Scouts could do a better job."

"We'll clean it up," Paris said.

"I hope so," Davies said. "Otherwise somebody's head goes on the chopping block. You're ranking detective here, Wade, and don't you forget it."

"I'm not in charge of the case," Paris said.

"You are and you're not. You're boxed in. If somebody has to take the rap, I don't have to tell you who it's going to be. You understand? That's the way they've set it up and I can't change it."

"I understand," Paris said.

"I'm glad I made it clear," Davies said. "You take it the way it comes. You're in no position to fight anybody. You can't afford to have Coyne bear you a grudge either. He fits with the people upstairs, and the way it shapes up he's liable to be your boss someday. You don't fit, Wade. Not since we've got this new administration."

"I know that too," Paris said.

"Sure you do," Davies said. "It's the old story. It isn't the job you do, it's who your brother is." He bent down and brushed some sand from his trouser leg. "Now I've got to go back to Capitol City and cool off the Governor and the Attorney-

General. That's the least I can do for you. You don't want them down here, too, do you, Wade?"

"No, I don't."

"You need anything?"

"Yes," Paris said. "Did Olsen have a family?"

"A wife," Davies said. "And there's a son who's a mate on a freighter."

"We'll have to see Mrs. Olsen."

"Coyne's already seen her. What do you mean *we?* You want me along?"

"Yes."

"Come on then," Davies said. "Let's get it over with."

It was a saltbox house with a high steep roof, the shingles on it bleached and unpainted. A neat little lawn, with a gravel path in the center of it, marked off with giant, white clam shells along either side. Inside, in the waxed-pine-paneled living room, Mrs. Olsen sat, heavy-faced, dry-eyed now, her hands clasped in her lap, eyes fixed, phlegmatic, stoic. The friends had moved out of the room, rustling in the kitchen, rattling dishes, pausing to listen.

Colonel Davies had moved over near the window. He picked up a small barometer and studied it. "You were saying your husband had no enemies, Mrs. Olsen?"

"No enemies, sir. Carl was a good man. Been here thirty-five years. I don't remember him fighting with anybody. He was a good-natured one."

Paris moved his chair into the light of the brass hurricane lamp. "Your husband knew Mr. Endicott, of course."

"Oh, he knew Mr. Charles since Mr. Charles was a baby. Carl would go fishing with him many times. He'd bait up Mr. Charles's own boat too. Mr. Charles always treated him kindly and generous-like."

"Last Monday night," Paris said, bending forward in the maple chair, "when Mr. Charles was killed, where was your husband?"

"Home with me. He was mending his shrimp net."

Davies put the barometer down. He frowned. "All night, Mrs. Olsen?"

"All night," she said.

"You must be mistaken," Davies said. "You think again. It was Monday night. Your husband was out in his boat."

"No," she said stolidly. "He was home."

"We have to be absolutely sure of that," Paris said. "If he was out in his boat that night, he might have seen somebody in an outboard motor. That's why it's so important. This person might have seen your husband and your husband might have recognized him."

"No," she said. "The other policeman, Mr. Coyne, asked me the same thing. Carl didn't leave the house that night, not once."

Davies frowned again. He picked up his hat and rolled the brim in his hands. "It's now Thursday," he said. "Your husband had a charter yesterday morning?"

"Yes. He went out early."

"What time?" Paris asked.

"Before eight."

"Who chartered the boat?" Davies asked. "Can you tell us that?"

"Carl didn't mention it," she said. "He did say it was a single."

"Since when does only one person charter a boat?" Davies asked.

"It doesn't happen often," she said. "Not unless the man is very rich. Carl gets forty-five dollars a day and furnishes the bait."

"And you don't know who chartered the boat?" Paris asked. "Did Carl give you a hint?"

"No," she said. "He didn't say a word."

Paris stood up. He went across the room and picked up his hat. "That person didn't charter the boat for fishing. You know that, Mrs. Olsen."

"I know now," she said quietly.

"Well," Davies asked Paris impatiently, "is there anything else you want to ask her?"

"No," Paris said. "That's what I had to know."

Davies went over to Mrs. Olsen and took her hand. "Thank you, Mrs. Olsen. We can't bring your husband back, but we're going to bring in his murderer."

They went out and walked down the path to the waiting police car. Paris looked out to sea, watching the waves come in.

"You all set now?" Davies asked him.

"Not all the way," Paris said. "I'll have to go back to Eastern City first."

"Then you run along," Davies said. "I'll go back to Capitol City and sit on the lid." He walked over to the car and got in. He ran the window down. "Keep me informed up to the minute," he called.

"Yes, sir," Paris said.

15

THE EARLY MORNING SUN, SHINING ON EASTERN CITY, threw long shadows across Kingston Street. The sun, rising higher, hit the police cars parked on either side of Number 311, glinting off the hoods and the windshields.

Inside Harold Dana's apartment the police technicians worked, sprinkling their gray fingerprint powder, gathering lint and dust in the hand vacuum cleaners. A man with a large wrench had uncoupled the bathroom pipes. In the living room another detective, chewing gum impassively, had an upholstered chair turned over and was feeling along the webbing.

Paris, in the kitchen, standing on a chair, was peering along the tops of the windows. Springer stood in front of the opened electric refrigerator, staring inside. He turned around as Hennessey came in from the bedroom. Hennessey shook his head slowly.

"I think," Springer said to Paris, "the guy isn't running. He's holed up somewhere, and he's planning to stay there for a while. Otherwise he wouldn't have prepared it by emptying and disconnecting the refrigerator."

Paris came down from the chair. In the corner of the kitchen near the door there was a small, enamel-painted wastebasket. He put it on the formica-topped table and began to rummage through it. Now he turned to Springer with a slip of paper in his hand.

Springer, watching him, came across the room and looked over his shoulder.

"It's a grocery list," Paris said. "You're right. The boy is holed up somewhere. Down at the bottom of the list it says *Gal of Ker.*"

"Who's the Gal of Ker?" Springer asked. "The only gal I know is Our Gal Sal."

"He planned it in advance," Paris said. "It was no sudden move. *Gal of Ker* is an abbreviation."

"Sure," Springer said. "I'm smart too. A gallon of kerosene."

"Yes," Paris said. "He wouldn't need kerosene in a rooming house or a hotel. It means he has a cabin somewhere."

"So you'll go look for a cabin," Springer said. "You'll go to the mountains. Even in July they need some heat some nights."

"It could be a beach," Paris said. "You get some cool nights when the east wind is blowing."

"You can count me out of this trip," Springer said. "Do you know how many mountain and beach resorts we have in this state? My corns hurt just thinking of them."

"The Danas might *own* a cabin," Paris said. "How long would it take to run through the Registry of Deeds?"

"I know how long," Springer said. "I've had sad experiences with them. They've got more red ribbon than Colton's Department Store. And what if the cabin is out of state? Why do you always have to do everything the hard way?"

"You're right," Paris said, putting the wastebasket down. "We'll talk to Judy Dana."

"Sure," Springer said. He looked down at the slip of paper on the table. "You've been too easy with her. By all that's right, she should sing like a canary now." He picked up the slip and looked at it reflectively. "Listen, maybe she thinks her brother is the killer. In that case she'll clam up good."

"We'll find out," Paris said. "You coming with me?"

"What else can I do?" Springer said. "I'm hogtied to this case."

They drove along Dudley Avenue and stopped in front of the white turreted house. Across the street a man in a detective car was smoking a cigarette. Springer opened his door and stepped out. The man, seeing him, flipped the cigarette into the street, stepped out of the car and crossed over. He came up to Springer and put a finger to his hat.

"You see anybody come in or out?" Springer asked him.

"No, Captain, it's been quiet. I've been on with Lenzetti since six this morning. He's out back. Nothing's happened."

"It's eight now," Springer said, looking into the car window at Paris. "She should be up."

"Yes," Paris said, getting out of the car. They went up the stairs together. As they came to the small porch, the front door opened. Judy Dana stood there, wearing a black skirt, white blouse and black-and-white spectator pumps.

"I've been waiting for you," she said intensely. "I called Police Headquarters. I want to leave this house. That man standing down there on the sidewalk near his car. He would have stopped me, wouldn't he?"

"Yes," Paris said.

"You can't keep me here," she said. "It's unconstitutional."

"Well now," Springer said, scratching his jaw. "That's a delicate point."

"You can't do this," she said, stamping her foot. "It's imprisonment."

"Now, now," Springer said, "don't get yourself worked up. The Inspector wasn't exactly holding you here. That *would* be unconstitutional. All he said was that he'd take you into custody if you left the house. He could have done that last night. He had reason to."

"I want to get out of here," she said. "I've got to find my brother."

"We want to find him too," Paris said. "Where were you thinking of looking?"

"I don't know," she said. "I swear I don't. But I must do something."

"Did Mr. Shapp call you last night?" Paris asked.

"Yes," she said. "Look, my brother isn't a criminal. Mr. Shapp explained that to me. He didn't steal that horse. You have no business with him any more."

"It's more than a little matter of a horse," Springer said gently.

"Your brother is hidden away somewhere," Paris said to her. "He's planned a long stay. Do you own a summer cabin, Miss Dana?"

"Yes. But we haven't used it since my father died."

"Where is it?"

"At Tacona Beach," she said. "You think my brother is there? Do you?"

"Where's Tacona Beach?" Springer asked.

Paris shook his head slowly. "It's funny how those things will work out," he said. "Tacona Beach is next to White Sands." He turned to Judy Dana. "What's the address?"

"It's Beach View Avenue," she said. "There's no number. It's a small, gray-shingled cottage with blue shutters. My father owned it since I was born. Of course that's where Hal would go. And I didn't even think of it. I'm going with you, Inspector."

"No," Paris said. "You stay here."

She shook her red hair. "I'm going with you," she said. "He's my brother and you're not going to hurt him."

"You'd better take her," Springer said to Paris. "We might need her at that. The brother might be as bad as she is when it comes to talking. This way I figure we've got ourselves a hostage."

"Perhaps you're right at that," Paris said. "All right, Miss Dana. Go get a coat."

"If it's next to White Sands," Springer said, "it's about eighty miles. I've got to call my wife first."

Paris drove fast. The car weaved through the heavy city traffic, siren sounding, then picked up speed on the shore highway. They wound their way through the beach towns, slowing up in the centers, continuing on again along the sand dunes and the water.

Paris looked across the front seat to Judy Dana. "You should have told us about this before," he said. "We've wasted valuable, essential time. I can't guarantee anything now."

"I had to do it that way," she said. "I had to lie. I just had to."

"Why?" Paris asked.

"Why? What other reason could I have? I had to do what I thought was best for Hal. Look, you must have a brother or sister, Inspector. You would know what family love is."

"I don't have a brother or sister," Paris said.

"Then a sweetheart," she said. "Somebody you love dearly."

"I don't have a sweetheart."

"He ain't that bad," Springer said from the back seat. "He was in love once."

"Nobody's interested in that," Paris said sharply.

"Okay, okay," Springer said, "I won't tell her." He leaned over to Judy again. "He's dog-tired, ma'am. He works too hard. This time he ain't slept in twenty-four hours. But he won't quit."

"Maybe he'll go home after this," Judy Dana said. "You *do* have a home, Inspector?"

"No," Paris said. "I travel most of the time."

"If it isn't one hotel," Springer said, "it's another."

"It must be a lonesome life," Judy said.

"Sure, it's a lonesome life," Springer said. "And it's a thankless life. But that state shield means more to him than anything. That's why he's so honest. I've never seen a cop as honest as him, ma'am. Not only outside, but inside too. And what good is it all? He's still caught in the system."

"You sound like you pity him," Judy said.

"I do. Sure he's got a State Inspector's shield, and him just being a kid too. But that's all he's got is his shield."

Judy turned to Paris. "And what are your ideas about this, Inspector?"

"I leave those to Captain Springer," Paris grinned. "The Captain thinks he's a homespun philosopher. I've resigned myself to him."

"It's because he respects my opinions," Springer said.

Paris looked at a road sign as they flashed by. "We're coming into Tacona Beach," he said. "Where's the cottage, Miss Dana?"

Judy sat up erect in the seat. "Take the first left turn," she said.

Paris slowed the car. He drove along a quarter of a mile. There was a yellow blinker at the intersection. He swung the car left and drove down the road a mile. They came to a small village, the main street bunched with stores, a tiny motion picture theater. They passed streets shaded with trees; then the streets began to thin out, running into dead ends. The road narrowed and the houses became sporadic.

"Turn left again," Judy said.

Paris turned the wheel at the next crossroad. The road led along the brush, curving in parallel to the beach. Bathers sat along the shore. There were beach chairs and striped umbrellas. Cottages hugged the sand. Paris passed them by.

"There," Judy pointed suddenly.

It was a tiny gray-shingled cottage with freshly painted blue shutters. It lay up close to the sand dunes. Peeking out of the side of it to the seaward, was the snout of a green car.

Judy moved to the edge of the seat. "That's Hal's car," she said.

Paris drove by quickly. There was a street fifty yards away. Paris turned the corner and parked the car.

Springer opened the rear door and stepped out. He moved under the shade of a tree, his eyes on the cottage.

"You stay here for the moment, Miss Dana," Paris said. He opened his door and slid out of the seat. He came around the car and met Springer under the tree. He studied the cottage, unbuttoning his coat jacket with deliberate fingers.

"I'll go now," he said to Springer. "Sam, I'll cross the road and go along the beach. You wait until I get there, then take the back. Cut behind these cottages and keep under cover."

"What's all this?" Judy said, leaning out of the window. "Why all these plans? Hal won't run away."

Paris ignored her. Springer reached inside his coat and took his gun from the shoulder holster.

"What are you doing?" Judy asked him. "Please? What are you doing?"

"That's all right, ma'am," Springer said. "You stay in the car for now. I've never met your brother. I want to get a look at him first and see if he's sociable."

"Please, Captain," she pleaded. "You don't need a gun. Hal is my baby brother. Please."

"Nobody's going to harm him," Springer said. "Not if he behaves. But we've got to be sure, ma'am."

Paris started for the corner. "You don't need a gun—" Judy was saying. Paris, his pace quickened, moved out of earshot. He crossed to the other side of Beach View Avenue and onto the beach, his shoes sinking into the sand. He went around a dune, past the half-covered reed grass. He ran now, closer along the water, where the sand was firmer. He cut across, moving diagonally to the front of the cottage.

He heard a voice behind him across the sand. It was Judy Dana.

"Hal!" she called. Paris turned and saw her. She was running along the sand toward the house, her skirt flying over her knees, the sand spurting up behind her high heels.

The front door of the cottage opened and a young man came

out onto the porch. His arm came up, shielding his eyes from the sun. He looked past Paris toward the girl.

"Judy!" he shouted. He ran down the stairs to meet her. Paris stopped. She came by him, her breath sobbing, and into the young man's arms.

Captain Springer turned the corner of the cottage and came out to the front, gun cocked.

Paris came up to him. "It's all right, Sam," he said. "You can put it away. Nothing's going to happen."

"I'm glad of that," Springer said.

Paris looked over at Judy and her brother. "Yes," he said. "Now I think we'll all go inside and talk."

16

IT WAS A PRIMITIVE ROOM WITH A HICKORY TABLE AND four straight-backed chairs, an old cretonne-covered lounge chair and a plaid-covered studio couch. The red brick fireplace was clean and empty. There was a square oil stove with a vent in the back of it, beside it a gallon jug of kerosene. In the tiny kitchenette there was an old icebox. A pile of washed dishes lay on the wooden sinkboard near a half-loaf of bread in a wrapper and a tin of luncheon meat. The bedroom door was open. The bed, square, wood-framed, showed a striped mattress and a padded quilt.

The four of them were in the living room. Against the wall, Harold Dana stood, his arms outspread, his face frightened. Bending in front of him was Captain Springer, patting his hands over the boy's clothes. Judy Dana watched silently. Beside her, face tired, eyes weary, was Wade Paris.

Springer straightened up. He turned to Paris. "I guess the kid's clean."

"All right," Paris said. "Let him sit down."

The room was quiet. Paris looked at Harold Dana, now sitting in a straight-backed chair, noticing the white knitted sport shirt, the unpressed brown slacks and the white sneakers.

"We know all about this Chinese horse," Paris said to him. He moved over and sat down in the lounge chair near the fireplace. "We know pretty near everything else. Now we want to hear what *you* have to say."

Harold Dana looked at his sister. Judy nodded her head. "It's true," she said. "They're not interested in what happened at the store. They want to find out who killed Mr. Endicott and the state detective."

Springer lifted his eyes. "There's William Lakos too," Springer said mildly. "That's Eastern City, and that's my jurisdiction."

Harold Dana's mouth moved. "Lakos is dead?" he asked.

"Yes," Paris said. "Don't you have a radio here?"

"No," Dana said.

"I want you to tell them everything," Judy said to him. "You don't have to keep anything back now."

Harold Dana rubbed his mouth nervously. "I didn't know Lakos was dead. Honest, I didn't. Do you believe me, Judy?"

"Of course, I believe you," she said. "Tell them, Hal."

"I was trying to do something decent, that's all," he said. "For once in my life I was trying to do the right thing."

Springer moved onto the studio couch. "What were you trying to do that was so decent, son?"

"I was going away," Dana said. "I knew it was rotten what I had been doing to Mr. Shapp. Don't think I didn't. I thought if I went away, Mr. Shapp would be rid of me. It would be best for him and Judy. But I needed money for the trip."

"But you couldn't go away and leave me," Judy said. "Where would you go, Hal?"

"Texas, Judy. I thought I'd get a job in the oil fields."

"Where did you plan on getting the money?" Paris asked.

"I didn't have any real plans then," Dana said. "Not until last Friday after the auction. Mr. Shapp was upstairs and I was unpacking the trunk we bought. There were some old newspapers at the bottom, all yellow and everything and dated 1908.

Underneath there was something wrapped in an old piece of flannel. I took it out and unwrapped it. It was the statue of a horse. Now I never saw one like it before and it wasn't like the other things in the trunk at all. Then I got the idea, right there. About the money, I mean."

"Where did you go with the horse?" Paris asked.

"I went straight to Lakos with it. I told him I wanted five hundred dollars for it. He laughed at me. I started to walk out. All the time he had his eyes on the horse. He stopped me at the door. He looked at the horse again. Then he said he'd give me two hundred and fifty. Then we argued. Then he said he'd give me another two-fifty if and when he sold the horse. He told me he was taking a chance, because the horse might not be worth a dollar."

"Where did all this happen?" Paris asked.

"In Lakos' office."

"What time?"

"Before noon, on Friday."

"So he gave you two hundred and fifty dollars," Paris said. "You signed a receipt for it. Was there a duplicate?"

"I have the duplicate," Dana said. "That's what made me suspicious. He gave me the money and made me sign the note for it."

"Why were you suspicious?" Paris asked.

"Because he never offered me that kind of money before, and not so readily. All those times I met him in the railroad station, he gave me fifteen or twenty dollars for things. Did you know I used to meet him in the railroad station?"

"Yes," Paris said. "How come you took both the money and the horse then and walked out of his office?"

"Because I was suspicious," Dana said. "I told him I'd better hold onto the horse until he made his contact. And when he made it, I wanted to be there. We argued about that too. Finally he laughed and said he trusted me and he had my note anyway. He was a funny guy. He had a very weak character."

"Let's not talk about weak people," Springer said crisply. "We know all about Mr. Lakos' character. What did you do then?"

"I went home," Dana said, his voice subdued. "I began to think. I remembered the Endicott Collection of Asiatic Art and I knew the Endicotts were at Sunset Point every summer. You can see the Point from here if you swim out a way. And I thought Mr. Endicott was the best man to see. In that way I could find out how much the horse was really worth. So I took it with me and drove over to see him."

"When was that?" Paris asked.

"The same day," Dana said. "Last Friday in the late afternoon. I took my car and drove over to White Sands Beach. There was a road to Sunset Point and there were two stone columns half-way down and a sign that said private road. There was a chain between the posts, but the chain was down. When I got near the house I saw a nice-looking man getting into a big, gray convertible. I asked him if he was Mr. Endicott. He said yes. I took the horse out of the box and showed it to him. I noticed he was a little excited about it. Then he asked me how much I wanted. I took a crazy stab, just to see his reaction. I said ten thousand dollars. He really surprised me when he said that would be all right. But there was a catch to it. He wanted me to leave the horse with him so he could check on it and see if it was genuine. He had a man named Mr. Noble who was going to look at it."

"You didn't go into the house with Mr. Endicott?" Paris asked.

"No, sir. We talked outside."

"Nobody else saw you there?"

"I don't know," Dana said. "I didn't see anybody. We were alone out there."

"You didn't know Endicott had a gun in the desk drawer of his library?"

"No," Dana said. "I don't know anything about a gun."

"All right," Captain Springer said. "You knew nothing about a gun. What else happened there?"

"I didn't want to leave the horse," Dana said. "I told **Mr.** Endicott I'd hold onto it. When Mr. Noble came, I'd return with the horse. Mr. Endicott agreed to that. He said he'd need time to make the arrangements. I told him he'd have to hurry, because I had other places to sell it."

"You were feeling pretty cocky then," Springer said, "weren't you?"

"Yes, sir," Dana said. "Then I was. But not now, sir."

"Well, I'm glad of that," Springer said. "Because there's nothing to be cocky about. You gave Endicott until Monday night. Is that it?"

"Yes, sir. I said I'd see him Monday night at ten o'clock. He agreed to that. I drove away."

"You drove away," Paris said. "You didn't see Mr. Endicott take down the license number of your car?"

"No, sir," Dana said, startled. "Did he do that?"

"Go on," Paris said. "What did you do then?"

"Well, to tell the truth, I was worried. That horse was really worth ten thousand dollars, maybe more. I never had anything so valuable in my life. I had to make sure I'd see him Monday night and nobody would stop me."

"What do you mean, son?" Springer asked. "Who would stop you?"

Harold reddened. "Well, Lakos would, if he found out. Judy certainly would too. She'd say it was wrong."

"So you hid out here in the cottage until Monday night," Paris said.

"Yes. But I had to go back to Eastern City first to get some clothes and bedding. Then while I was in Eastern City I bought some groceries too, and some oil for the stove. I didn't want anybody to see me walking around White Sands Beach. Then when Monday night came I drove over to the Point."

"Now this part is very important," Paris said. "What time was it when you drove over to the Point?"

"Well, I left here about ten after nine. I thought I'd drive there and look around first. I got to White Sands Beach maybe twenty past nine. I hung around the boat basin, watching Sunset Point Road. I didn't see anything until half-past nine. Then a car drove by me and headed up the road to the Point. An old guy with a red face and white hair."

"He was alone?" Paris asked.

"Yes," Dana said. "I thought that would be Mr. Noble, the man Mr. Endicott had talked about. I waited five minutes. Then I started up the car and drove down after him. When I came along the cliffs I saw three cars parked near the house. But one of them had a flashing red light going. I knew it was a police car and I thought Endicott had set a trap for me. I turned the car around and raced back here. Just in time too. Because when I came to the four corners, two State Police cars tore by me, heading towards Sunset Point. I got back to the cottage and I've stayed here since."

"Why?" Paris asked.

"I was scared. I didn't know what was going on. The next morning I went down to get a newspaper. I saw Mr. Endicott had been murdered. Then I got really scared because they'd think I had something to do with it. Then I didn't want Lakos to get his hands on the horse. I knew he'd be around Eastern City looking for me."

"Didn't you have an idea Judy would know where you were?"

"No, sir. I didn't think so. We haven't come to the cottage for two years, since Dad died. We needed the money so we'd been renting it. This year we thought we'd use it ourselves weekends. But we hadn't had a chance to get down here."

"And that's the whole story?" Paris asked.

"Yes, sir. I was only staying here until things straightened out. I didn't kill Mr. Endicott. I wasn't near the house that night."

"All right, son," Springer said, uncoiling his long body and getting up. "Where's this horse?"

"I've got it here," Dana said. He stood up and went into the tiny kitchenette. He went to the sink and opened the oak cabinet underneath. He took out a cardboard carton and brought it into the living room. He put it on the table. The box was sealed all around with gummed paper tape. He ran a thumbnail along the top of it, splitting the paper. He lifted the sides of the box top. There was a mass of shredded paper. He delved down deep.

He brought out the statue of a horse, shreds of paper clinging to it. The statue was twelve inches high and made of buff-colored pottery, vividly splashed with blue. The neck of the horse was arched and the mouth was open and on its back it carried a high saddle. The head harness was decorated with plum blossoms and there was a palmette-shaped pad between the eyes.

Springer stared down at it. "And that's worth ten grand?"

"That's what Mr. Endicott wanted to pay," Dana said. "The horse is twelve hundred years old. There's beautiful workmanship there."

"Yes," Springer said, his voice hardening. "There's beautiful workmanship all around here. Especially in your story. You mean to tell me you never knew Mr. Noble before?"

Dana's face became peaked. "No, sir."

"You never heard of him?" Springer asked.

"No, sir."

"You mean to tell me you hadn't gone to him and cooked up a little deal between you?"

"What kind of a deal, sir?"

"You know what kind of a deal," Springer said. "He'd come along and tell Endicott the horse was worth a lot of money. Then the two of you would split the dough."

"No, sir," Dana said.

"Maybe I'm wrong," Springer said. "Maybe you had it cooked up with Victor Konstanz. Now you know who Mr. Konstanz is. Don't tell me you don't."

"Yes, sir," Dana said. "Mr. Konstanz is the biggest art dealer in town. But I never met him."

"Maybe I'm wrong again. Maybe the whole thing was planned between you and Lakos. Lakos sent you over to Endicott."

"No, sir. Mr. Lakos had nothing to do with it."

"Well, you weren't in on this thing alone," Springer said. "You can't make me believe that."

"Yes, sir," Dana said emphatically. "I was alone. Mr. Lakos had seen the horse, but he didn't send me to Mr. Endicott. I did that myself. Nobody else knew about it."

Springer ran a hand over the back of the statue. He looked at Paris. Paris nodded.

"Okay, Harold," Springer said. "Now I think the Inspector wants to tell you something."

"Yes," Paris said. "We're going to take the horse for the time being, Hal. I'll give you a receipt for it. And I'll also have to take you along with it. You'll be locked up in the county jail at Waretown."

Judy Dana flounced out of her chair. She faced Paris. "You're going to do *what?*"

"I'm sorry," Paris said. "Your brother is linked up with four murders. I've got to hold him."

"You'll do no such thing," she said. "My brother has done nothing."

"You listen to me," Paris said. "Up to now, two people outside of your brother have seen that horse. Both have been killed. A cop who was about to see it was killed too. Another man has been washed up on White Sands Beach. Do you want Harold to be next, Miss Dana?"

There was a quick flush to her cheeks. "That's ridiculous," she said. "What else are you going to tell me? That there's some silly ancient curse attached to this horse?"

"No," Paris said. "It's nothing of the kind. There's a murderer running around loose, that's why. This murderer doesn't care who's in the way. We can't afford to gamble with anybody, Miss Dana. Not even your brother."

"You can't make me believe such nonsense," Judy said. "I know why you're doing it."

"No, ma'am," Springer said. "Let me tell you something else. The Inspector got too close to this killer himself. He was shot at too."

"You mean the inspector was shot at?"

"Yes, ma'am. So if you've got that much faith in your brother, you'll be glad to see he's put safely away. If he's not the killer, then he's sure better off inside the county jail than outside."

Judy stared down at the statue on the table. "I don't know," she said slowly. "Do you want to do it, Hal?"

"I guess I've got to," Harold said gloomily. "They don't leave me much choice, do they?"

"It's the best way," Paris said. "We'll drive you over to Waretown and find some minor charge to hold you on."

"Not you, Wade," Springer said. "I'll do that. You stay here with Miss Dana. Get some rest. I'll pick you up on the way back. Then we can drive Miss Dana to Eastern City." He turned to Judy Dana, rubbing the back of his neck. "Do you have a place where the Inspector can take a nap?"

"Thanks, Sam," Paris said. "But I don't need a nap. All I want is some time to think."

17

"YOU DOZED OFF," JUDY SAID. "RIGHT IN THAT CHAIR." Paris rubbed his eyes and sat up. His hands came away from the chair arms. "I didn't mean to," he said, looking at his watch.

"You slept only half an hour," Judy said from the studio couch. She tucked her legs under her. "At first I was sitting here boiling mad. I wanted to hate you. And I almost succeeded in doing it."

"Why did you want to hate me?"

"You sent my brother to jail, didn't you? Without a qualm or a quiver. It didn't mean a thing to you. Not a thing." She grimaced. "I wouldn't want a job like yours for all the money in the world. I wouldn't be able to live with myself."

"But you're wrong," Paris said. "A cop has to do those things, whether he likes it or not. That's the job. He doesn't make the laws, Miss Dana. He just carries them out. What would *you* have done in my position? Taken Harold's word for everything?"

"I'd have made sure of my ground first."

"It isn't always easy," Paris said. "But you said you wanted to hate me. What changed your mind?"

"I don't know." She hesitated. "I watched you sleeping. You didn't look very cruel or hardboiled. You looked more like a tired little boy. A very tired little boy. Are you *r e ally* so tough, Inspector?"

"No," Paris said. He stood up and stretched. "I don't know how I gave you that impression."

Judy smiled. "When you're awake, you have a protective covering. I suppose it's only superficial."

"I guess some cops do acquire a thick skin. You can't blame them. They don't come in contact with the best things in life."

Judy bent down and slipped her feet into her pumps. She stood up and went to the window. She moved the curtain aside and looked out. "When is the Captain coming back for us?"

"He won't be long."

She turned around quickly. "They won't do anything to Hal?"

"No, I'm sure they won't."

"Why are you so sure? Are you the boss?"

"In a small way."

"Then I feel better," she said. She came over and smiled up at him. "I don't know why, but now I trust you, Inspector."

"Thanks," Paris said, patting her arm. "And I trust you."

"Splendid," she said. "As long as there's such a nice mutual feeling, let's go out and bask in the sun. There are some beach chairs on the porch."

Paris had put the reclining chairs side by side on the sand. Judy, her legs bare, her shoes off, flexed her toes in the warm sun. She leaned back in the chair, shaded her eyes and looked across the blue water. Now she turned to Paris. "Are you enjoying it?" she asked.

"I sure am," Paris said, rolling up his shirt sleeves and un-knotting his tie.

"The company too?"

"Yes." Paris grinned. "The company especially."

"I'm flattered. I think you could act like a human being if you let yourself go. Have you ever tried it? Have you ever done this before?"

"This?"

"Sat with a girl alone. The Captain said you were in love once."

"Yes," Paris said briefly.

Judy bent down and sifted the sand through her fingers. "Was she pretty?"

"I thought she was very pretty."

"And you broke off with her?"

"*Now* what are you doing?" Paris asked. "Questioning me?"

"You questioned me enough," she said, holding her hand up and letting the sand trickle out. "What's the matter? Why are you afraid to talk? Can't you take it, Inspector?"

Paris grinned. "People are always asking me that. Do I ask so many personal questions?"

"You certainly do."

"And you think it's your turn?"

"It's only fair. Don't you want to be fair, Inspector?"

"All right, I'll be fair. What do you want to know, Miss Dana?"

"Judy," she said. "I can't talk to you if you're going to be so formal."

"Judy," Paris said.

"That's better," she said. "Now what terrible thing happened to make you so hard and bitter? What did this girl do to you?"

"Now wait a minute. She did nothing to me. She was a very fine girl."

"Where did she come from?"

"Eastern City."

"What was her name?"

"I'm not going to tell you that, Judy."

"Why shouldn't I know her name?"

"Because she's married now."

"Oh," she said. "But you were engaged to her first?"

"Yes, I was."

"Why did you break up?"

"For one thing," Paris said, "I wasn't much of a suitor. I work out of the Attorney-General's office and I'm all over the state. I was out on assignments most of the time. She got tired of waiting for me, and I don't blame her. Well, she met somebody else. Somebody who had a sensible occupation. A man who would come home every night, who could offer companionship where I couldn't. She wrote me she had learned to love him. That's how it happened."

"I'm sorry to hear that," Judy said. "I think she made a mistake."

"No, it was best for her. I had no right to even consider it. It would have been no life for a girl. There would always have been a packed bag near the front door."

"But if she loved you—"

"Love is like a garden. It has to be cultivated."

She smiled. "You sound like a poet. It's the oddest thing."

"Why?"

"Well, you're a policeman. Policemen don't talk like poets." She made a circle in the sand with a bare toe. "Of course, I never met a policeman before. And I always thought the world would be better without them."

"Why do you think that?"

"I don't know. Mostly because folks hate authority and policemen are a challenge. People resent restraint and they'll defy the law because of that. Perhaps if there were no police there would be no incentive for crime. Did you ever think of it that way?"

"It's not a new theory," Paris said. "It's anarchism. There was a Frenchman named Pierre Proudhon. He conceived that idea over a hundred and fifty years ago. He thought it would work."

"Well, wouldn't it? After all, we do have thousands of years of civilization behind us. My goodness, we don't need policemen to watch us."

"There was a police strike in Boston in 1919," Paris said. "For three days there wasn't a cop on the streets. The people tore at each other like wild animals. I think they would have destroyed the city and also themselves, if the militia hadn't been called in." He scuffed his feet along the sand. "You see, civilization works both ways. The more civilized we become, the more criminal we become. Our jails were never larger, our homicide rate never higher. That's what civilization has done."

"You sound discouraged," she said.

"We progress," Paris said wryly. "People are better educated than ever. They're smarter. Science has made great advances. So has the criminal mind. That's improved too, like everything else."

"And this case you're working on," Judy said. "Is that an example?"

"Yes."

"And you have no idea who's behind it?"

"I have some ideas on it," Paris said steadily. "We're up against a very clever person. Here I've been sitting, talking to you. Yet all this time I've been trying to puzzle out how a person could be in two places at the same time. And I don't believe in magic either." He twisted his head around toward the road. There was the sound of a car driving up and of brakes squealing. Paris stood up.

"It's Captain Springer," he said to her.

She stood up, turned and looked at the car. "He's alone," she said faintly.

'Don't worry about Harold," Paris said. "He's going to be fine where he is. Come on, we'll drive you home. We're going back to Eastern City anyway."

18

THE OFFICE WAS ON THE TWENTIETH FLOOR OF THE NEW-
est skyscraper in Eastern City. The pebbled glass door said
Law Offices; underneath, *George S. Hanft, Jerome Woodstock,
Nicholas R. Sears.* Inside, the air-conditioned reception room
was paneled in light wood. There were gay modern prints on
the walls. Near the door was a row of green leather chairs. There
was a desk with a young woman behind it. The girl smiled
briefly and professionally at them.

"Mr. Hanft," Paris said to her.

"Do you have an appointment?"

"No. But tell him it's Inspector Paris."

"Mr. Hanft is in conference," she said. She smiled mechani-
cally again, turned and plugged into her switchboard. Paris
stood there. The girl turned back. Her eyebrows lifted. "Mr.
Hanft," she said, "never sees anybody without an appointment."

Springer took off his hat and put it on the desk. "You tell him
Captain Springer is here too," he said. "We know each other."

The girl's hand came up and patted the bun at the nape of her
neck. "Well," she said dubiously, "I'll try."

She plugged into the board again, pressed down a lever and
spoke into her mouthpiece. She nodded at them. "It's the first
door on the left."

They moved across the blocked rubber-tile floor. There was a
bleached oak door, and on it, in gold letters, was *George S.
Hanft.* The door opened. A middle-aged woman came out and
closed it. She was wearing a light summer suit and flat-heeled
shoes. She looked at them from behind her rimless glasses and
went by. Paris knocked and opened the door.

The office had short-piled carpeting in severe gray. There
were gray drapes at either side of the large casement window.
The desk was large and kidney-shaped. It held a gold-colored,

square desk lamp, a leather-trimmed desk blotter, a white onyx pen set and two telephones. There were glassed-in bookcases that held volumes of red, gold and tan bound law reports. Hanft swung his big leather chair around and stood up. He reached out a hand to Captain Springer. Springer came to the side of the desk and took it.

"Hello, Captain," Hanft said gravely. "It's a pleasure." He looked by Springer. "And you, Inspector Paris. Glad to see you again. Sit down, both of you." He opened a desk drawer and brought out a lacquered box. "Cigars. Help yourself."

Springer took a cigar. He sniffed at it and put it into his breast pocket. "Thanks," he said. "I like to smoke them after dinner. I hope you don't mind, Counsellor."

"Not at all," Hanft said, sitting down again. "Well, I suppose you have some kind of news for me."

"We're making progress," Springer said. "I kind of feel we're in the home stretch."

"Good, good," Hanft said.

"We came to ask a favor," Springer said.

"I hope I can grant it, Captain."

"We'd like to get hold of the Endicott inventory."

"What inventory is that, Captain?"

"The storage pieces," Springer said. "We need the list. I understand you have a copy of it."

Hanft frowned and moved his hands along the desk. "Yes, there's a copy of it here," he said slowly. He adjusted the leather-trimmed blotter. "But I see no reason why you should have it. It has no bearing on the case."

"There is a bearing," Paris said. "We wouldn't ask for it otherwise."

"That's not good argumentation, Inspector. I don't conduct a legal practice on generalities. This list is the property of the Endicott estate—of which I'm counsel and Mrs. Endicott is administratrix. And as counsel, I can't turn the list over to you."

Springer moved in his chair. "I think you can trust Paris and me."

"It's not a question of trust, Captain. You're dealing with an estate now. There are certain laws protecting estates."

"What reasons do you have for refusing?" Paris asked.

"I have a lot of reasons," Hanft said. "When you have publicity seekers such as you have in this case, the list will get into the hands of the wrong people. There is personal property involved here. Something I've always considered sacred."

"We need a break on this, Counsellor," Springer said.

"I'm sorry," Hanft said. "The answer has to be no. Now, was there anything else you wanted to talk to me about?"

"No," Springer said. "It looks like we'll have to get a court order, Counsellor."

"That will take time," Hanft said. "I'll fight any court order."

Paris stood up and went to the desk. "We can't waste time," he said. "We need the list today. Now."

"That's out, Inspector," Hanft said briefly.

"Then I'll have to phone Mrs. Endicott," Paris said.

"I don't think you should do that," Hanft said.

"I'm doing it," Paris said.

"She buried her son today," Hanft said. "This morning. I was at the funeral with her. I saw the condition she was in. Knowing all that, you'd phone her now?"

"Yes. Because it's her son I'm thinking of."

"I wonder," Hanft said.

"I'd still like to use your phone," Paris said.

"I can't refuse you," Hanft said. His voice was brittle. He got up and moved away from the desk. "The operator knows her number."

Paris picked up the telephone. He spoke. There was a pause. He spoke again. He looked over at Hanft and held out the telephone.

Hanft came back to the desk and took the phone. He spoke to Mrs. Endicott. Suddenly he put the phone down. His face was mottled in red.

"She's seldom gone against my advice," he said to Paris. "I don't know what kind of a hold you have over her."

"She wants the killer brought in," Paris said.

"Are you inferring I don't?" Hanft snapped. "What I object to is this poking around into personal affairs. I say it's not necessary. You're floundering around without purpose."

"There's purpose," Captain Springer said, standing up. "Do you have the list, Counsellor?"

"You'll get your damn list," Hanft said angrily. He pressed a button under the desk. Paris moved away. The door opened and the middle-aged woman came in and stood just over the threshold.

Hanft said, "Miss Koslo, I want the inventory on the Endicott storage pieces. It's in the file safe. Would you bring it in, please?"

Miss Koslo looked sharply at Paris. Then she nodded. She went out, closing the door softly. They waited silently. The door opened again and Miss Koslo came back with a green cardboard folder. She put it on the desk. Hanft opened it and riffled through the papers. He closed it, fastened a large paper clip to the top, and handed it to Paris.

"You'll find it all there," he said. "Miss Koslo will make out a receipt for it and you'll sign it. I want it back as soon as possible."

"We'll do that," Paris said, putting the folder under his arm. "Thanks, Mr. Hanft."

But Hanft had stood up. He had turned his back and was looking out the window. He didn't answer.

They drove through the intown traffic, the hot sun beating down on the roof of the car. At Police Headquarters they pulled up at the red-painted curb. They went up the broad stairs and through the old granite archway. The service elevator took them down into the basement. There was a dark, cool corridor and an acrid smell of disinfectant. At the end of the corridor was the custodian's office. They came up to the caged door. The man sitting behind the small metal desk heard their footsteps and

looked up. He was wearing faded green denims with a police
shield pinned to the breast pocket.

"Hello, Maguire," Springer said.

Maguire stood up. He had a pale, unshaven face and his short,
clipped hair was gray and bristly. He scratched his grizzled
jaw. "Hello, Captain," he said. "You want to come in?"

"Yes," Springer said. "I want to look at the Lakos stuff."

Maguire unlocked the heavy door. Paris and Springer stepped
in. They followed Maguire down between the steel partitions.
There was a row of open steel bins with numbers on them.
Maguire stopped. "This is Lakos," he said.

On the shelf of the bin there was a large pewter urn with a
tag tied to it. There was a battered steel cashbox, a folded black
alpaca coat with a torn sleeve. There was a fountain pen, a set of
six flower-patterned, English dinner plates, an old portable typewriter, some newspaper clippings with an elastic band around
them, and two small statues.

"This all they brought from Lakos' office?" Springer asked.

"There was money too," Maguire said. "They found that in
the cashbox. They've got that put away upstairs." He wiped
a pair of watery eyes. "They say there was thirty-five thousand
bucks in that little box."

Paris held up one of the dinner plates and put it down. He
picked up the newspaper clippings and shuffled through them.

"What are those papers?" Springer asked.

"Notices of auction sales," Paris said.

"The Kolloway auction in there?"

"Yes," Paris said, "and a lot of others." He put down the clippings and picked up the pewter urn. He turned it over and
looked at the base. Now he set the cardboard folder on the shelf.
He looked through the typewritten pages. He shook his head.

"No?" Springer asked him.

"No," Paris said. "There's a silver water bottle listed. But
this one isn't silver."

He pushed the urn aside and picked up one of the tagged

statues. He held it up to the light of the electric bulb. It was a copper-colored figurine about six inches high; a man with an Oriental face tilted to one side, and wearing a large headdress. He was seated on a throne with his legs squatted. He leaned on one arm. The other arm was on his knee. The throne had a carved oval back.

"What's this thing made of?" Springer asked. "Gold?"

"No, it's either copper or bronze," Paris said. He opened the cardboard folder again and ran his finger down a crisp parchment page. "Here," he said. "Bodhisattva, Diëng, Java. Copper. Five and a half inches high. Tenth century."

Springer stared at him. "You reading that from the list?" he asked softly.

"Yes," Paris said.

"What's Bodhisattva?"

"I don't know," Paris said. "But it's down here. Sam, this statue is from the Endicott Collection."

Springer grinned at him. "It's good you're such a stubborn cuss, Wade. Now we're getting somewhere." He reached for the other statue. He turned the tag around. It was the figure of a woman and it was carved from gray stone. She had a smiling, benign face. She was nude to the waist. There was a crown on her head, and a necklace around her throat. Her right hand was up as though in a blessing.

Paris turned a page and studied the typewritten sheet. "Vishna," he read. "Kashmiri, India. Stone. Eight and a half inches high. Ninth century." He looked up. "That seems to be the closest description to it, Sam."

"Don't ask me," Springer said. "We need an art expert and we need one fast. Who've you got that's handy?"

"You know who," Paris said. "You'd better phone Victor Konstanz and tell him we're coming over. We'll bring these along."

"Captain," Maguire said, "you'll have to sign for these things."

"I'll sign for them," Springer said. "Get the slip ready, while I use the phone."

A cooling breeze had come up and small white clouds moved
-across the sky. The wrought-iron sign above the entrance to
Konstanz' creaked and swung gently back and forth. Paris
went up the stairs and opened the door. Behind him was Captain Springer holding a brown cowhide briefcase. Inside there
was a quietness, then a sound of padded footsteps across the
carpeting. Mr. Jelkes came to meet them.

"Mr. Konstanz is expecting you, sir," he said to Paris. "You
can go right up."

They went up the wide staircase to the second floor. The office
door was open. Victor Konstanz sat behind his desk. He smiled
bleakly.

"Good afternoon, Inspector," he said. "From the phone call
I got, your visit sounds urgent."

"It is," Paris said. "This is Captain Springer of the Eastern
City Police."

Konstanz leaned forward and shook hands. Springer said,
"Hello, Mr. Konstanz." He put the briefcase down on the desk.
He opened it and brought out the two statues.

Paris said, "Do these look familiar to you, Mr. Konstanz?"

Konstanz picked up the copper figure. He turned it over in
his hands. "This looks like a Bodhisattva."

"Would it be Javanese? Tenth century?"

"Yes," Konstanz said. "I think it is."

"Have you seen this particular figure before?"

"I think I have. Ten years ago, as I recall. I bought it in New
York and sold it to the Endicott Collection. That is, if it's the
same one."

"It must be the same one," Paris said. "This statue is on the
Endicott list. What's a Bodhisattva?"

"It's a figure representing the virtues of Gautama Buddha,"
Konstanz said. "One of the symbols of Buddhism. I'm not sure
which one it represents."

"It's listed as being tenth century," Springer said. "Maybe
it's a copy. This doesn't look to me as being a thousand years
old."

"It's copper," Konstanz said. "It's been restored by electrolysis. Very easily done too. I'll guarantee the authenticity of it. I sold it. I don't sell copies, Captain."

"What about this stone statue of the woman?" Paris asked.

Konstanz looked at it. "That's a Vishna," he said. "I don't think I sold that to the Endicotts. I'm sure I didn't."

"What's a Vishna?" Captain Springer asked.

"A different cult," Konstanz said. "Brahman. One of the three deities. The other two are Brahma and Shiva. This Vishna, or Vishnu, has many incarnations. It's a complicated religion, Captain."

"Thanks," Paris said. "Do you know where we found these, Mr. Konstanz?"

"No, I don't," Konstanz said. "Did you borrow them from the museum?"

"No. They were found in the office of William Lakos."

Konstanz leaned back heavily. His fat jowls shook. "Surely you're joking. You said William Lakos?"

"Yes," Paris said. "Are you surprised?"

"Of course I'm surprised," Konstanz said. "I was reading about Lakos' death this morning. What would these statues be doing in his office?"

"That's what we thought we'd ask you," Captain Springer said.

"You're asking me something I don't know."

"Have you ever had business dealings with William Lakos?" Paris asked.

"Don't be foolish, Inspector," Konstanz said. "Lakos always dealt in junk. He did try to sell me something once. But it was almost worthless."

"What did he try to sell you?"

Konstanz thought for a moment. "It was a long time ago," he finally said. "I don't remember."

"He never tried to sell you anything valuable?"

"I didn't know he handled anything valuable."

"How about a pewter urn?" Paris asked.

"Pewter urns are a dime a dozen," Konstanz said.

Springer picked up the statues and began to put them into the briefcase. He said, "You think Mr. Endicott could have given these statues to Miss Wyman?"

Konstanz moved his shoulders slightly. "He could have. But I think Miss Wyman would have liked something more practical. Say, something in the line of jewelry."

"Do you know a Harold Dana?" Paris asked.

"Who?"

"Harold Dana. He's a partner of Abe Shapp's."

"I've known Shapp for a long time," Konstanz said. "Although I don't see him very often, I did see him at the Kolloway auction with a young man. I didn't know he had acquired a partner. Was he the young man?"

"Yes."

"I didn't meet him."

"All right," Paris said. "Can you get away now, Mr. Konstanz?"

"Away? Where?"

"We'd like you to come down to White Sands Beach with us."

"Now?"

"Yes."

"Why?"

"It's very important," Paris said. "And it has to do with the Endicott case. I know you'd want to be the first to co-operate, Mr. Konstanz."

Konstanz's mouth tightened. "Naturally, I'll do all I can. But it *is* short notice."

"But you'll come?"

"Yes, yes, of course."

"Thank you," Paris said. "Now may I use your phone?"

Konstanz sat back and waved his hand. Paris took the phone from the desk and dialed the operator. "Capitol City, please," he said. "A collect call to Colonel Davies at State Police Headquarters. Detective-Inspector Paris calling."

He waited. Captain Springer snapped the briefcase shut.

"Hello," Paris said. "Colonel Davies? Look, I'm in Eastern

City now, but I'm going back to White Sands. I'll need the
Coast Guard. Yes, sir. One of their patrol boats. Yes, a boat. Can
you get one for me?" He shook his head impatiently. "No, sir,
not here in Eastern City. At White Sands. I can meet them at
the boat basin. Yes, sir. I should be there in an hour. I know it's
unusual, Colonel, but I need them. Fine. Thanks, I'll call in from
there."

He hung up and put the phone back on the desk. Konstanz stared at him with a puzzled look on his face. Paris said,
"You ready, Mr. Konstanz?"

Konstanz nodded slowly. He stood up and went over to a
wall cabinet. He brought out a white panama hat. His hands
trembled.

"What are you so nervous about, Mr. Konstanz?" Springer
asked.

"Of course I'm nervous," Konstanz said. "Since when have
I ever been taken along by the police? I'm a peaceful man."

"We're all peaceful," Springer said. "Peace is wonderful. But
this shouldn't take long."

"Let's say a prayer on that," Paris said, going to the door.

19

IT WAS NOW FIVE O'CLOCK IN THE AFTERNOON. THE
weather had changed abruptly. The wind, shifting to the
east, had cooled the air. Low clouds scudded across the sky, pil-
ing up layers, darkening. The wind, freshening, brought a few
scattered raindrops.

Paris, coming into White Sands Beach with Captain Springer
and Victor Konstanz, drove to the center of the town. The
Town Hall was white, with large round pillars in front, a tall
white steeple, a bronze Civil War marker, a World War I me-
morial and a World War II roster. The entrance was wedged
with people.

Paris parked the car. They got out. A girl came out of the crowd. She was wearing a tan polo coat and a white silk turban was wrapped over her blonde hair. It was Karen Wyman.

"Oh, hello, Victor," she said to Konstanz. "What on earth are you doing here?"

"Hello, Karen," Konstanz said, taking off his hat. "I've been invited."

"And there *you* are," she said, turning to Paris. "I've been waiting ever so long. I must talk to you." She looked at Captain Springer. "Alone, please."

"I'm busy, Miss Wyman," Paris said shortly.

"But I must talk to you," she said. "It won't take a minute. There's a drugstore across the street. Buy me a cup of coffee, Inspector."

Springer said, "Go ahead, Wade. You need a cup of coffee. You're dead on your feet."

"All right," Paris said. "You take Mr. Konstanz with you, Sam. I'll see you in the Chief's office."

"There seem to be a great many people around," Konstanz complained. "I would just as soon wait in the car. If you don't mind, Inspector."

"As you wish," Paris said. He started across the street with Karen Wyman. She linked her arm in his, the wind sweeping her perfume toward him.

The drugstore was crowded. Paris squeezed through to the counter and ordered two cups of coffee. Karen Wyman stood behind him. The coffee came. A booth emptied. Paris brought the coffee over. He pushed aside the soiled paper napkins and the crumb-spattered plates. He put the cups down on the wet table. Karen Wyman slipped into the booth. She took out a compact and ran a lipstick over her mouth. She smiled. Paris sat down.

At the counter, a man with black curly hair and gold-rimmed glasses was watching them. He swung his stool around, got off and came over. He leaned into the booth.

"Hello, Inspector," he said.

"Hello, Goyette," Paris said.

Goyette nodded to Karen Wyman. "Hello, Miss Wyman."

She smiled prettily. Paris said, "This is Eugene Goyette. He's with the Eastern City *Times-Herald*."

"Oh, a reporter," she said. "But I'm not talking to reporters."

Goyette looked by her. "What's up, Inspector?"

Paris said nothing. He put a spoon into the sugar bowl, filled it, put it into the coffee and began stirring.

"We're getting tired o' writing Coyne's pap," Goyette said. "He's making a lot of noise, but he hasn't got a thing. We're all four pulling out of here."

"It's a free country," Paris said.

Goyette said, "Don't be so hard to get along with, Inspector."

Paris sipped at his coffee. Goyette said, "We've had a lot of boloney thrown at us up to now. Suddenly everybody's clammed up. There's something in the wind, and I think you're at the bottom of it. It couldn't be Coyne. He's like that brother of his. If he had something, he'd crow like a rooster. You going to give out for us, Inspector?"

"I don't handle the publicity," Paris said.

"We know that," Goyette said. "But we know where the work is being done. I saw you with Springer. Give out, Inspector."

"I'm sorry," Paris said.

"Nothing?"

"Well, not yet," Paris said. He hesitated. "All right, hang around. I think something's going to break."

"When?"

"Very soon now."

"You're on the level?"

"Yes," Paris said.

"There's a Coast Guard boat in," Goyette said. "Are they part of it?"

"Yes," Paris said.

"Then I'll stick around," Goyette said. "Thanks, Inspector. Good-bye, Miss Wyman."

"Good-bye," Karen Wyman said. Goyette left the booth and went to the door. Karen Wyman picked up her coffee. She touched the cup to her lips.

"It's all very mysterious," she said to Paris. "You must tell me all about it, Inspector."

"What did you want to see me about, Miss Wyman?"

"It's about myself," she said putting the cup down. "You must have a horrible opinion of me." She smiled archly. "I'm not *that* bad, really."

"I'm sure you're not," Paris said.

"Do you get to Eastern City often?"

"Fairly often."

"That's nice," she said. "I come from Eastern City. Maybe we'll see each other again."

"Maybe," Paris said. "What is it you want, Miss Wyman?"

"You must do me a teensy-weensy favor," she said. "You must let me go home. I'm staying at the White Sands Hotel and everybody just stares and whispers. It's very disconcerting."

"I'm not keeping you here," Paris said.

"It's that Lieutenant Coyne," she said. "He won't let me go. You must speak to him."

"I have nothing to do with it," Paris said. "Is that all, Miss Wyman?"

"No, that's not all. They've had Walter down at the Town Hall and they've questioned him remorselessly. And they've asked *me* the most intimate, repulsive questions. How long am I going to put up with it?"

"Not long," Paris said. "By the way, Miss Wyman, did Mr. Endicott ever give you any gifts from the museum? Some small statues, for example?"

"No, he never did," she said. "And I don't know a thing about that Chinese horse either. Charles mentioned it to me, but that's as far as it went. And Walter and I never left the cottage that evening. You must believe me, Inspector."

"I do," Paris said.

"As for Walter," she said, "I never want to see him again.

He hasn't been chivalrous at all. He did nothing to protect my name. He's nothing but a grasping, evil person. I'm glad I found out in time."

"I'm happy for you," Paris said. "And I think you'll be free to go home by the time the day is over. Now if you'll excuse me, I must go."

He got up from the booth, went to the door, and out to the street.

There was a railing through the center of the Chief's office, dividing it in half. Behind the railing, Lieutenant Coyne was talking peevishly to a State Police sergeant. Near the door, Captain Springer sat in a chair smoking a pipe. Paris crossed the room, swung the small gate open and came through.

Coyne moved to meet him. "I've been waiting for you, Wade," he said. There was an edge to his voice. "I'll have to release a statement on the Dana kid."

Paris said, "We're not ready yet on Dana. I'll let you know when."

"We've got the kid, haven't we?" Coyne said. "The Commissioner's been calling from Capitol City every ten minutes. He wants you to phone him right away."

"I'll call him," Paris said. "What's the M. E. report on Olsen?"

"He died before hitting the water," Coyne said. "A fracture at the base of the skull. No water in his lungs. He wasn't dead more than a few hours. No robbery. He had money and papers on him."

"Nothing new on his movements?"

"No. He definitely didn't leave the house at any time Monday night. Whoever chartered the boat yesterday morning, did it by telephone. Nobody's come forward with anything."

"You know what time they left the basin?" Paris asked.

"A little before eight in the morning. Al Coats and a state trooper came by the harbor and saw the boat on its way out. They could see Olsen at the helm. The passenger was hidden from sight. Purposely or not, we don't know."

"Purposely," Paris said.

"So we canvassed the whole area," Coyne said. "Nobody knows who the passenger was." He took out a cigarette, lit it impatiently. "Where's the reason for it? Why this fisherman? His murder is the most senseless part of it."

"No," Paris said. "There's sense to it."

Coyne drew on his cigarette, taking the smoke deep into his lungs. "The Dana kid's behind the whole thing. But somebody worked with him. It was an inside job. That I'm sure of. Whoever he worked with, knew the Endicott house, knew about the Magnum revolver in the desk drawer, knew when Mrs. Endicott takes her walk. He had it timed exactly. But who? Almieda? I had him down here and sweated him plenty. I took the starch out of him, but he swears he's clean. The girl puts on such an innocent act, I'd like to smack her one. I still think there's a love or jealousy angle there."

"No," Paris said. "If they wanted to rid themselves of Endicott, all they'd have to do was go away. I think it would be a week before Endicott knew they were gone."

"Okay," Coyne said. "Who else? Henry and Lizzie Davis? I got after them too. This Henry Davis is slow with his answers. I had to nudge him a little."

"You're too free with your hands," Paris said. "I don't want you nudging anybody."

"Somebody's got to open up," Coyne snapped. "I'm sick of this polite business."

"No nudging," Paris said coldly. "That's out. Now you wait a minute, while I put the call through to the Commissioner."

He went over and spoke to the uniformed trooper at the telephone. The door to the office opened and Chief Kay came in. He went directly to Paris. Paris shook hands with him and they walked back to where Springer was sitting.

"Inspector," Kay said, "I don't like the way they knocked Henry Davis around."

"I'm sorry about that," Paris said. "But I've stopped it. It won't happen again."

"They had no reason to," Kay said. "Henry would tell them

anything they wanted to know. That's no way to do things, going around beating up people. And take these newspapermen. They're swarming all over town, bothering the residents. They think this is a picnic. It's no picnic to the town, Inspector. What do you think these killings are going to do to the tourist business?"

Captain Springer shifted his legs. "Probably increase it," he said. "You know how people are, Chief. It's a known fact that there are bigger crowds at a fire or accident than there are at a chess match. Most folks are sadists."

"Then there's a Coast Guard boat at the basin," Kay said. "Did you order that, Inspector?"

"Yes," Paris said. "I called Colonel Davies. He got it for me."

"The Chief Boatswain's Mate said he's waiting. He wants to know how long it'll be."

"Not long," Paris said. "I want you to do something for me. I want you to find an old friend of Carl Olsen's. Somebody who would know his fishing habits and the route he'd take. Do you have anybody like that?"

"Yes," Kay said. "There's Clem Dahl. You want me to get him?"

"Yes," Paris said. "I'll meet him down at the boat basin. We're going out on the Coast Guard boat."

"You going out to look for something?" Kay asked.

"Yes," Paris said.

Kay took off his cap and scratched his head. "That's a damn big ocean out there. You'll find that out quick."

"It's not that big," Paris said. "And it's got a bottom."

"I'll get Clem Dahl," Kay said. He went across the floor and opened the door. He bumped squarely into a small, fat, agitated man. The man bustled by Kay and came into the room. He looked around.

Coyne, seeing him, went up and said, "Hello, Mr. Ramspak."

Ramspak snorted. "What the hell's going on around here?" he asked. "*I'm* the chief law enforcement officer in this county. I demand to know what's going on behind my back."

"Nothing's going on, Mr. Ramspak," Coyne said. "Paris just got in and he's been giving me the facts to date."

Ramspak whirled on Paris. "I want to talk to you, Paris," he said. "You've got that Dana kid locked up in Waretown. You put out a dodger on him last night. Now I find he's in my jail. Nobody told me a thing about it."

"We wanted to keep it quiet," Paris said. "We need a little more time."

"Look, Paris," Ramspak said, "you don't even belong here. You've been sent by the Attorney General in an advisory capacity. I'm the D. A. here. This is my show and I'll run it. And I don't like the amount of authority you take in your hands either."

"I've taken no authority in my hands," Paris said.

"You have,"Ramspak said. "When you come into my county, I've got to know what goes on. You get that straight, once and for all." He spun around to Coyne. "You're working under *me,* Paul. Why didn't you tell me about the Dana boy?"

Coyne said, "I found out only a couple of hours ago, when Paris called in from Eastern City. I had to digest the information first and report it to the Commissioner."

"That's nice double-talk too," Ramspak said. "But I'm 'way ahead of both of you. One of my assistants has been squeezing Dana in his cell. The boy did some talking. What do you think of that, Paris?"

"I don't think much of it at all," Paris said.

"I feel sorry for you," Ramspak said. "And I'll tell you this. You're not going to whisk the boy out of there and hold him in Eastern City."

"I had no such intention," Paris said.

"He stays where he is," Ramspak said. "I'm going to charge him in the morning."

"With what?" Paris asked.

"The Endicott and Hallmark homicides. Eastern City can wait on the Lakos killing. I've got first crack at the boy. I'll bind him over for the Grand Jury. And I want that statue too, Paris. That's evidence."

Captain Springer stood up. "Mr. Ramspak," he said, "you going to give the newspapers a statement now?"

"Why not?" Ramspak snapped. "This is the biggest case the state ever had. We've got millions of people waiting for word on it. You don't realize the pressure I've been under. I've had two Congressmen and a U. S. Senator at my heels."

"We've all had pressure," Paris said. "But you can't charge the boy. He's not your man."

"I'll chance that," Ramspak said. "I can always release him."

"You don't understand," Paris said. "He's only a boy. A first-degree murder charge is a hard thing to live down. Even if it's dropped later, the boy will always carry it with him."

"Don't tell me *my* business."

Captain Springer, his hands deep in his pockets, nodded. "Mr. Ramspak," he said, "ain't you in an awful hurry on this?"

"You keep out of it, Captain," Ramspak said.

"Sure," Springer said. "It's none of my affair. But it seems to me it's kind of soon to be running for governor. If I was you I wouldn't start my campaign till next spring."

Ramspak's face darkened in color. "That's enough out of you, Springer. I'm going to turn in a report on you for that."

"Now that's too bad," Springer said. "I've been a cop over forty years. If somebody's going to turn in a report on me at my age, maybe it's time for me to retire."

"Maybe you should have, a long time ago," Ramspak said.

"All right," Springer said. "You listen to me, Mr. Ramspak. I'm a lot older than you, and maybe I ain't as smart. But you bust this thing before it's ready, and you'll run into trouble."

"Who's going to give me trouble, Springer? You?"

"No, not me," Springer said. "But Paris and I have got this thing all set up, and nobody's going to dump the apple cart. If you want to tip it now, go ahead. But you'd better be absolutely sure what you're doing. Because if you're wrong, you're going to be laughed at. I know politics. I've had to dirty *my* feet too. And I know this. It's all right if you're in office and you don't do nothing. Then your voters have got no cause to find. But if you do something and it's laughed at, then you're finished. I've seen plenty of politicians laughed out of office. You make a wrong move here and they'll laugh at you so hard, you couldn't get a vote as dog-catcher."

Ramspak, his face brooding, tapped a foot impatiently. He looked around the room. "Well," he said finally, "I'm reasonable. We don't have to stand here and argue about it. You say you want time. How much time do you want, Paris?"

"Four or five hours," Paris said.

"I'll give it to you," Ramspak said. "But you'd better come up with something. Otherwise the laughing will be on the other side."

Ramspak went over and put his hand on Coyne's shoulder. "I didn't mean to get mad at you, Paul. We've always co-operated together. It's these two who got me so sore. Your brother knows how I feel about you."

He turned around, glared at Paris, then went out. The office door slammed. Springer fished for his pipe and filled it slowly from the pouch. His face was grave and thoughtful. The state trooper left the desk and came to the gate.

"Your call to the Commissioner is ready," he said to Paris.

Paris took a deep breath. He went through the little gate and over to the desk. He picked up the telephone. "Hello," he said.

The Commissioner's voice answered him. "Where the hell have you been all day, Paris? And why didn't you contact me?"

"I've just got in from Eastern City," Paris said. "I phoned Coyne with the information."

"Well, I'm leaving for Waretown now," the Commissioner said. "Are we ready to close this thing up, Paris?"

"I think so," Paris said.

"That's better. Much better. Now we'll move. You've got that horse statue with you?"

"Yes, I have it."

"Good, good. Did you get a confession out of the boy?"

"No, sir," Paris said.

"We'll work on him. I've got just the man who can do it. How about the sister? You have her in custody?"

"No, sir. I've sent her home."

"You've sent her home? Alone?"

"No. The Eastern City Police are watching her."

"I can't understand you, Paris. We don't want this thing to get away from us and have the Eastern City cops move into the limelight. I'd better get the newspaper people in now. At the same time I'll get some of my own men into Eastern City and pick the girl up. We've done all the work on this. I can't have Eastern City hog anything."

"Captain Springer has been working with me," Paris said.

"That's okay. We'll see he gets a mention."

"Let me explain," Paris said. "There's no sense in everybody trying to crowd to the front. This isn't a question of publicity."

"What's the matter with you, Paris? You getting disillusioned or something?"

"No," Paris said. "I've been a cop too long to become disillusioned. I know what's going on. I'm trying to tell you this. The Dana kid is clean. He's the wrong one."

"What?"

"He's the wrong one, Commissioner."

"This is a fine time to tell me that, Paris. You feeling all right?"

"There's nothing wrong with me," Paris said. "I've got the boy in custody merely for his own protection. I've told Ramspak that."

"You mean you don't have anything after all?"

"No, I've got something. I'm not absolutely sure yet. But it's going to take a few more hours."

The phone was silent for a moment. Then, "Well, if I didn't know you better, Paris, I'd think you and the Colonel were trying to pull something. If you've got any ideas along those lines, don't try it, boy."

"I'm not trying to pull anything," Paris said coldly. "I'm just trying to wind up the job."

"All right. But I want the wire open all the way. The minute it cracks, you get through to me. Understand?"

"I understand," Paris said softly. "I understand too well."

He hung up. He went through the gate. Springer, sitting in the chair now, puffed methodically on his pipe. Springer crossed his high black shoes and looked up.

"Seems like all the vultures are out today," Springer said. "I can hear them flapping their wings from here. There'll be trouble when they get through picking on the bones. Somebody's bound to get left out. And he'll be the one who'll do all the hollering. We've made great strides in human progress, Wade."

"Yes." Paris smiled. "Maybe we both should have become streetcar conductors."

"We'd be obsolete there too. Time changes things. They're using buses now."

Lieutenant Coyne came over, putting on his hat. Paris turned to him and said, "Springer and I are going out. I've got Victor Konstanz in my car and I want to leave him here. Will you keep an eye on him?"

"Tell somebody else," Coyne said shortly. "I'm going over to Waretown and talk to the Dana kid."

"You don't have to talk to him," Paris said. "I'll talk to him all right," Coyne said. "You've been too soft with the kid, Wade. When I get through with him, he'll tell me who was in on the deal."

"You'll keep your hands off Dana," Paris said.

"You telling me something, Wade?"

"Yes," Paris said.

Coyne studied him, his arms slightly flexed. "What's wrong, Wade?" he asked. "You grandstanding? You making a play for the sister?"

Paris started for him. Springer lunged up and came between them. His arm came up and blocked Paris.

"That's not the way to do it, Wade," Springer said softly. "Not here."

The room was quiet. Faces turned toward them. Somebody scraped a chair. Paris brought his hand up and rubbed his knuckles slowly.

"You're right, Sam," he said. He looked at Coyne. "All right, Lieutenant. We'll do it this way. I'm ordering you to keep away from Dana."

"You're doing what?" Coyne said.

"It's an order, Lieutenant. Do I make myself clear?"

Coyne stared at him, his face a mask. "You make it clear, Inspector," he said. "But I'm going over your head, Inspector. I'm calling the Commissioner."

"You'll do it through channels, Lieutenant. You'll clear it with your supervisor first."

"The Commissioner isn't going to like it, Inspector."

"You'll call Colonel Davies first," Paris said.

"I'll call him," Coyne said, moving away to the telephone. "I'll call him now, Inspector."

Paris looked over at Captain Springer. "All right, Sam," he said. "If you're ready, we'll go down to the boat basin."

"I'm ready," Springer said. "I want to get out of this formal atmosphere here. But I hope we know what we're doing."

"This has to be it," Paris said. "It's the only chance there is."

20

THE SKY HAD COMPLETELY CLOUDED NOW. THERE WAS A strong northeast wind and the sea was choppy and white-capped. Paris, \driving to the boat basin with Victor Konstanz and Captain Springer, saw the white, eighty-three-foot Coast Guard patrol boat moored to the wharf. He pulled in along the pier. He stepped out, Springer following. The waves came in past the breakwater and hit against the pilings. The patrol boat, motors idling, moved up and down with them.

Chief Kay came over. There was a man with him, small, wizened, tanned, wearing a peacoat and a brown cap.

"This is Clem Dahl," Kay said to Paris. "He's an old friend of Carl Olsen's. He knows the sea better than anybody around."

Paris shook hands, introduced him to Captain Springer. A state trooper shooed some children away.

Paris said, "You can wait for us in your office, Chief. I'd also appreciate it if you took Mr. Konstanz along with you."

"I'll do that," Kay said. "Good luck."

They left Chief Kay and went up the gangway. The Chief Boatswain's Mate, cap askew on his head, buttoned his dark-gray windbreaker and signaled to the sailors at the bow and stern. The sailors cast off. The motors revved. The boat backed out slowly, showing the black numbers on the prow.

The boat swung slightly and moved out through the yacht basin. Paris, in the bow, near the canvas-covered six-pound gun, introduced Clem Dahl to the Chief Boatswain's Mate.

"He'll give you the course," Paris said.

"It's going to be rough out there," Dahl said, looking up at the sky. "It's a fresh northeaster. You head out straight between the markers."

The Chief Boatswain's Mate nodded his head and shouted to the bridge. He turned to Paris. "How about the grapplers, Inspector? When do you want them out?"

"We ought to clear the channel first," Paris said. "What do you think, Mr. Dahl?"

"Sure, it's too soon," Dahl said.

"All right," Paris said. "Now where do you think Olsen went yesterday?"

"He must have taken his party bottom-fishing," Dahl said. "That's best this time of year. The tide being what it was yesterday morning, his best bet was off Balsam's Ledge. He'd get himself some good-sized cod there. That's where they feed."

The boat moved along, passed the breakwater and mounted the choppy seas along the bluff. To the right of them, the deserted Endicott house became larger.

They passed the Point, the wind sweeping in on them. Paris put up his coat collar, bracing himself. Dahl said, "Set your course south by southeast."

The Chief Boatswain's Mate called to the quartermaster behind the glass of the small bridge. The boat veered sharply, heeled, picked up speed. The spray hit along the bow, wetting the passengers. Captain Springer moved to the lee of the bridge, grumbling something and reversing his pipe bowl.

"What's wrong?" Paris called to him.

"Plenty," Springer said glumly. "I don't like boats. They don't agree with my stomach."

The patrol boat forged ahead, hull vibrating under the increase in speed. At the stern, a sailor worked on a bridle with a six-foot length of pipe. Chained to the pipe were four grappler hooks, each fifteen inches long. The sailor uncoiled the manila rope attached to the bridle. He lit a cigarette with cupped hands and waited.

The Chief Boatswain's Mate had gone topside to the bridge. Dahl called out to him. "Take a bearing on the Point. Keep it over your left shoulder, maybe two degrees. You got about two miles to go."

The boat changed course slightly. Springer moved behind the bridge, his back to the wind. Paris, his legs wide apart, stared ahead. Ten minutes went by. The Endicott house had shrunk in the distance.

"We're off Balsam's Ledge," the Chief Boatswain's Mate called. "You want the hooks down now, Inspector?"

"Yes," Paris said. "Get them over. I guess the rest of it is up to you."

"Okay," the Chief Boatswain's Mate said. He shouted to the sailor in the stern. "We'll use the ladder pattern on it."

The boat swung around, motor throttled down, stopped, drifted. The sailor in the stern cast over the grapplers. The boat moved under way again, slowly, at a speed of two knots.

Paris teetered along the deck to the stern. He stood there watching the sailor at the grappling hooks. Another sailor in a windbreaker came aft and moved up alongside. Paris waited. Twice the grapplers fouled in the rock and the boat backed to free them.

An hour went by. Toward the east, on the horizon, the sky had darkened considerably. It had grown much colder. The sailors at the stern had been relieved by two others. Springer, huddled now behind the bridge, had his pipe in his pocket and his hands in his coat sleeves. Paris, anxious, fretting, paced along the narrow deck, looking at his watch.

A sailor called suddenly from the stern. "We've latched onto something."

The boat stopped, idled, drifted slightly. The grapplers came up slowly. Paris, besides the two men, leaned over the edge of the boat, watching carefully.

A burlag bag came up, dripping mud, slimy. It came aboard. A seaman stood by and hosed it off with sea water. Paris, his pocket knife out, bent down and slit the bag. He pulled it apart. Inside was a small metal chest. There was a steel clasp on the lid. Paris unfastened it. Springer, alert now, moved alongside.

"Is that it, Wade?" he asked.

"Yes," Paris said, opening it. "It's the wire recording machine."

"You think it'll work now?" Springer said.

"No. The tubes are ruined inside. But the spools are going to be okay. They're stainless steel.

"I'm glad of that," Springer said. "Let's get out of here and back onto dry land."

"Yes," Paris said. "This is the end of it."

21

THE BOAT HAD DOCKED. THE RECORDING MACHINE HAD been put into the trunk of the police car. Paris stood on the wharf, watching as the boat went under way again and started for its base. Paris turned now and got into the waiting car. The crowd thinned away.

The police car left the beach and sped along into town. It was beginning to rain. Along the streets the people moved to shelter. It was dark enough now for the store lights.

In the Chief's office at the Town Hall, Victor Konstanz sat stolidly in a chair, smoking a long cigar.

"I'm sorry to have kept you waiting so long," Paris said to him. "But we won't take up much more of your time."

Konstanz rolled the cigar in his mouth. "I still don't know why I'm here."

"I can tell you that now," Paris said. "I have the T'ang horse in the car and I'll need your opinion on it."

Konstanz took the cigar from his mouth. "Then I can forgive you for keeping me waiting. I'd like very much to see it."

"You will," Paris said. "I want Mr. Noble to look at it too. Chief Kay is phoning him now." He looked over to the desk behind the railing. "Is everything ready, Chief?"

"It's all set," Kay said. "Where's Springer?"

"He's outside waiting," Paris said.

"Then let's go," Kay said.

John Noble was waiting for them. He shooks hands with Victor Konstanz. They chatted for a moment. Victor Konstanz expressed sympathy.

It had grown fully dark and the lights were on. They crowded into the tiny apartment. Chief Kay, as usual, stood near the door, his thumbs through his holster belt. Noble sat down on the sofa, straightening his seersucker coat jacket, moving the cushion slightly under him, waiting, his pink face bland, yet urgent and expectant. Konstanz sat across from him in a rattan chair. In the corner, near the bedroom, Springer put the briefcase between his legs and sat down. He leaned back, his eyes half-closed.

Paris picked up the cardboard box and brought it to the coffee table in front of the sofa. He put the box down on it.

He lifted the flaps and brought out the statue of the T'ang horse. Konstanz stood up quickly and came over. He picked it up and ran his fingers along the surface, his eyes studying the arched neck. He turned and held the statue to the light of the floor lamp. He swung around again and extended the statue to John Noble.

"What do you think, John?" Konstanz asked.

Noble pursed his lips, looked at the statue, reached out and took it. He felt the texture of the pottery with his fingertips. He put it slowly into the box again.

"It looks like T'ang to me," he said to them. "You, Victor?"

"Yes," Konstanz said. "I should say it was genuine." He smiled at Paris, moved back to his chair and sat down. "John Noble and I have been disagreeing for years. Though it was mostly about prices."

"But you agree this time?" Paris asked.

"Yes," Konstanz said. "This is one time we're in accord."

Noble put his hands up. "Now I'm not positive," he said. "I don't like to commit myself. I'd have to take some tests first."

"I think that can wait," Paris said. "We've got four murders to wind up first."

"I understand," Konstanz said, starting to get up. "If you don't need me any more, I'd better go."

"No, stay a moment," Paris said. "I want you to hear this. It's been a peculiar case. There have been four murders, all connected. One of the victims was Charles Endicott, millionaire art collector and philanthropist. Another was a State Police lieutenant. Then we have a small-time crooked art dealer with a large bank account. And last, an obscure fisherman. Yet all of them were linked together, one and inseparable." Paris stopped and looked at John Noble. "Why?"

"I suppose if you knew that," Noble said gently, "you could solve the case."

"Yes," Paris said. "The important thing is that one of the victims was a cop. Secondly, Carl Olsen was killed almost under the very eyes of the law. The murderer moved along and through the police, and yet he left no clues. I would call him a very clever man."

"And a brave man," Konstanz said seriously.

"Yes," Paris said. "A brave man. I don't begrudge him that either. But more importantly, he was a methodical man. A man who had set a plan. A man who, once he set the plan into action, wouldn't stop. Lieutenant Hallmark wouldn't deter him. He had planned on that too. It made no difference how many people were around. In fact, the man did better than that. He used the police as an alibi. That's how clever this man was."

The room was silent. Noble cleared his throat. "I can agree with you there, sir," he said, nodding his head. "It would have to be an ingenious man."

"It was," Paris said. "Because he was talking on the telephone when the Endicott murders were being committed. Next door to him the local Chief of Police was playing cards." Paris walked over to the wall near the telephone and tapped it. "This is thin beaver board. From the next apartment the Chief of Police and five others could hear this man talking on the telephone. The man couldn't have a more unimpeachable alibi."

Noble moved slightly on the sofa. His mild blue eyes came up. "You're talking about me," he said to Paris.

"Yes," Paris said. "But you weren't talking on the telephone the time the murders were being committed. At that time you were shooting down Lieutenant Hallmark and Charles Endicott."

Noble chose his words carefully. "We're not that far advanced in science that I could be in two places at the same time."

"No," Paris said. "At the time Chief Kay heard your voice from here, you were in the Endicott library. You used a wire recorder. Chief Kay heard a record of your voice."

Noble shook his head sadly. "Farfetched," he said. "That

would be a physical impossibility. I couldn't very well set the recorder and at the same time be at the Point two miles away. The recorder wouldn't go on by itself."

"It did go on by itself," Paris said. "You have a clock radio here. You set the clock radio at a blank channel for nine o'clock. You attached the wire recorder to it. A moment before nine o'clock, the clock radio went on. It set off the wire recorder. And that was your conversation with Mr. Hanft."

"It's a beautiful theory," Noble said. "You mean I didn't use the telephone here?"

"No," Paris said.

Noble spread his hands. "Well, then," he smiled. "It doesn't stand up. How was Mr. Hanft able to talk to me at the same time? A telephone conversation goes both ways."

"That's right," Paris said. "You *were* actually talking to Mr. Hanft over the phone. But not this phone here. You were in the Endicott library then. You knew the Lincolns were at the Hanft house, so you were safe using their outboard. You sailed to the Point, docked the boat and came up the landing to the terrace. Once inside the library you kept your eyes on your watch. At nine o'clock you excused yourself and used the phone for a moment. You stepped behind the desk, dialed Hanft and spoke briefly to him. When you were through you hung up. You shot Mr. Endicott and Lieutenant Hallmark from behind the desk."

"And what would I use for a weapon, Inspector?"

"You had the Endicott gun in your pocket. The same gun you had used on Lakos earlier in the day. The gun Mr. Endicott was so upset about because he had found it missing from the drawer. Do you want more, Mr. Noble?"

"Yes," Noble said, "I want to hear how foolish a person can sound."

"I'll tell you how foolish," Paris said. "You went back the same way you came, with the boat. You tied the boat up at the basin and went up the fire escape to your room. At twenty-five minutes past nine, you left your room again. You drove over to the Endicott house once more. But that was the second time you'd been there that evening."

"It's so preposterous," Noble said, his pink face trembling, "that I won't even answer it. Because why on God's earth would I want to kill Mr. Charles? What possible motive could I have?"

"All right," Paris said. "We'll talk about motives. We'll talk about a man who worked in the museum for twenty-five years. A man whose whole life was devoted to his job. A man whose job meant more to him than anything in this world. A man who would kill to keep that job, he had so much love for it."

"Then all the more reason why I would never do such a monstrous thing."

"No," Paris said. "Because there were the storage pieces. Most of them are gone now. You sold them through William Lakos. Wouldn't that be a motive, Mr. Noble?"

"It's the most ridiculous thing I ever heard," Noble said.

Captain Springer scraped his chair. He bent down and un-latched the briefcase. He took out the little copper figure. Paris went over and took it from him. He stepped back across the room and handed it to Noble. "Do you recognize this?" Paris asked him.

Noble looked at it quickly and put it down on the table. "It looks like a Bodhisattva."

"Yes," Paris said. "And it's part of the Endicott Collection. We found it in Mr. Lakos' office."

"You're making a grave error," Noble said. "It's not part of the Endicott Collection. I never saw this particular Bodhisattva before."

Paris turned his head to Victor Konstanz. "Mr. Konstanz?" he said.

"This is very painful to me," Konstanz said slowly. "I've known John Noble for many years." He looked steadily across at the sofa. "You know that's not true, John. That's an Endicott piece and there's no denying it. I have records of its sale to the

Collection. I have a photo of it in my files. I'm sorry, John, but facts are facts. I would have to testify to that under oath."

Noble twitched his mouth. "Very well. Supposing, as you say, Inspector, I *did* sell the storage pieces. Mr. Charles wasn't interested in them. He had agreed to pay the tax on them and Mr. Hanft would have no reason to have the inventory checked. It would never be discovered. And I still had no motive."

"Not then," Paris said. "Not until you spoke to Mr. Lakos last Friday evening. When he told you about a young man and a T'ang horse. He wanted you to examine it to see if it was genuine, didn't he?"

"I don't see any connection," Noble said.

"At the time, there wasn't. Not until Mr. Endicott called you in and told you the boy had been to see him too. *There* was the connection. And especially when Charles Endicott had the registration number of the boy's car and showed it to you. Then Monday morning he told you he was calling the police. That's when you had to act."

Paris stopped. He looked at Noble. The pale-blue eyes had become large and unfocused.

"You acted," Paris said. "You had to. Once they found out about the boy, linked him with Lakos, they would begin to probe. Lakos would talk. They would find out all about your dealings with him. So you had to be audacious. You had to make a clean sweep. Lakos was easy. You took the gun, went over to his house and shot him.

"All right, Lakos was gone. But that wasn't enough. The person who had the boy's license number had to go too. That was Charles Endicott. And when Lieutenant Hallmark arrived, that meant him too. You got the license number out of the wallet. But there was still the key to it all—the boy. You had to get him too."

Noble looked by him at Captain Springer. Springer, his face old and tired, shook his head. He pointed a finger at Noble.

"You didn't get the boy," Springer said. "He was hidden out. You waited at the apartment for him, but he didn't show.

That's when you took a shot at the Inspector. You were getting panicky then. It's too bad too. Because the boy wasn't two miles away from here the whole time. He was holed up at Tacona Beach. That would make it kind of funny, Mr. Noble."

"It's all theoretical," Noble said stubbornly. "You haven't shown a shred of evidence. Are you blaming me for the fisherman's death too?"

"Yes," Paris said. "And I'll agree it was all theoretical. I saw the clock radio the first time I was here. And after we had the Dana boy and knew he was in the clear, we still didn't have enough evidence. The copper figure helped. But it proved merely larceny, not homicide. True, we had motive. We could take the clock radio, go into court and present it along with the story of the recording machine. But it would be theory, not evidence. The only evidence would be the gun and the record machine itself. The gun could be disposed of easily enough. However, the machine was bulky. You could drive off and bury it somewhere, but there was the chance the police would trail you.

"So you made the move yourself. You were going to dump the machine in the ocean. You thought the ocean would be big enough. All you had to do was hire a boat and go fishing. The wire recorder was in the burlap bag and Olsen could have thought it was your fishing gear. Well, Olsen took you out to the fishing grounds. You started to throw the sack overboard. Olsen saw it, thought it was your gear, and tried to rescue it with a gaff. You got panicky for the second time. You hit Olsen over the head with the butt of the gun and threw him overboard. Then you took the tender in. Was that how it happened, Mr. Noble?"

Noble's eyes came up, fixed and staring. "The Coast Guard," he said. "The boat down at the basin. You went out with them?"

"Yes," Paris said. "The ocean isn't so big. The coast is charted. It's like a road map. We found the machine, Mr. Noble. We have the spool. Is there anything else you want to say?"

Noble didn't answer for a moment. "No, nothing," he said finally. "Only that I should have exercised better judgment in disposing of the machine. That was a very bad mistake."

"You made a previous mistake," Paris said. "You made your big mistake coming to the Endicott house at nine-thirty Monday night. The time when you acted so surprised that Mr. Endicott was dead."

"I'm afraid I don't understand," Noble said.

Captain Springer hitched up his chair. "What the Inspector is trying to tell you," he said, "is that a telephone conversation works both ways. You'd prepared for that. But you forgot that a thin wall works both ways too. If the Chief could hear your voice in here, then you could surely hear Al Coats when he came running in next door. You could hear him tell Chief Kay that Endicott and another man were dead. But you acted kind of shocked and surprised about it a half-hour later."

"Yes," Noble said wearily. "I fully understand now. Of course I wasn't in my room then. So I had no way of knowing what went on."

"Well, if you're ready," Paris said to him, "I think we can go now."

"I don't know what the museum will do," Noble said. "There is so much work. There is the recataloging that I've undertaken. There are the exhibits, the planning of additional space. Somebody will have to do those things, sir."

His hand moved away from his lap and darted in between the seat cushions. The big snout of the Magnum came up in his grip. Konstanz shouted, dropped to the floor, and began to crawl away. Springer, half-rising from the chair, reached quickly inside his coat. Chief Kay, from the door, his gun out, fired two shots, the explosions reverberating through the tiny room.

Noble slid forward, sighed, the gun dropping, his head hitting the top of the table. Springer came up quickly and lifted his head. Paris, over them, picked up the legs and laid Noble down on the sofa.

"He didn't mean no harm this time," Springer said. "He was pointing the gun at himself."

Kay looked down at the barrel of his revolver. "I didn't know," he said. "I was kind of watching for him to pull something. Then I seen the gun come out from under the cushion."

Paris went to the telephone and called the operator for an emergency doctor. Konstanz, on his feet now, ran for the bathroom.

Captain Springer knelt down. He took out his handkerchief and folded it hard and square. He pressed it against Noble's chest. The handkerchief was soon stained bright red.

"That's arterial bleeding," Springer said. "This man won't last till a doctor gets here." He pressed harder. "I think that D. A. is going to be disappointed as hell. There's going to be no trial."

Paris put the phone down. He looked over at Kay, who was still holding the gun tightly in his hand. Kay shook his head.

"The first time in my life I shot a man," he said softly. "The first time. I been out at the target range enough. But I never fired a gun at nobody."

"That's all right," Springer said to him from his kneeling position. "You didn't know what he was going to do. And if he *had* to be shot, maybe it was best you did it. It's your town, and it was really your show. Those other cops came in and made a big spectacle and pushed you all over the place. And when the showdown came, they weren't even here. You're going to get the publicity, Chief, and you don't need it. I'm a funny guy. To me, that's justice."

Victor Konstanz came in from the bathroom, gulping at a glass of water. He sank down into a chair and unfastened his collar.

"You don't look so good," Springer said to him. "But you just rest a while. It'll pass."

"I'm stunned," Konstanz said. "Good Lord, John Noble was the last person I dreamed of who could do such a thing. Anybody but John Noble. Why? Where's the rhyme or reason?"

"We get them like that once in a while," Springer said. "Why, I had a case once where the guy was a bookkeeper. He was a timid little guy who didn't weigh more than a hundred pounds, and he was always on the verge of crying. He was married about twenty-five years and he had a big wife. One day he cut her into pieces and buried her all over the back yard. *Why* he did it, I'll never know. I don't figure them. Paris does. He'll give you the big words."

"You can figure some of them," Paris said. "They do have a name for this one. Epileptic furor. It usually happens with a mild, recessive man like Noble. Maybe he was brooding inside about injustices. Maybe Noble's pay wasn't big enough, and he wouldn't bring himself to talk to the Endicotts about it. I don't know. Anyway he started to take things. It was his means of getting back. Then when he was about to be caught, he struck out. And the odd part is that, after he subsided, he'd probably never again harm a living thing. That's as much as I know about it. I'm not a psychiatrist."

Springer stood up. "And I'm not a doctor," he said, rubbing his stained fingers. "But I know one thing. Your man here is dead."

22

THE AIR WAS WARM AND THE SUN WAS STRONG AGAIN, and the waves came in frothing, subsiding gently and rolling onto the yellow sands of Tacona Beach. In front of the cottage, Judy Dana, in a tight little black lastex swimsuit, lay on a striped beach towel. Harold Dana, in dark blue trunks, splashed out of the water and stopped short at the edge. He waved.

Paris, driving up in the State Police car, waved back. He parked behind the little green sedan.

Judy Dana stood up and ran her hands quickly through

her red hair. She ran up the sand to meet him. Paris stepped out of the car and took off his hat.

"Hello," he said. "This is a nice weekend, isn't it?"

"Yes," she said. "And we're honored by the unexpected company."

"I thought I'd drop by and tell you the news," Paris said.

"Good news, Inspector?"

"Yes," Paris said. "I've been speaking to Victor Konstanz. He'll handle the horse for Mr. Shapp. On a commission basis. He'll get all he can. Mr. Konstanz said he might get seven or eight thousand dollars."

"It's wonderful news," Judy smiled. "All that money for a pale-looking horse. We're rich."

"Well, I don't know how rich that is in these times. But somebody's share will be a good little nest egg, if he doesn't run to the dog track with it."

"He's talking about me," Harold said, coming up and rubbing his head with a beach towel. "Not me, Inspector. I've taken the cure. Judy told me she'd take a switch to me if I ever did that again. And you don't know my sister. She'd do it too."

"I think she would." Paris grinned. "Well, that's all I had to tell you. I've got to go along now."

"Oh, not yet," Judy said. "Please. My aunt is inside and I know she'll want to see you."

"She's blaming our aunt," Harold said. "What are you being so coy about, Judy?"

"Don't be childish, Harold," she said, turning red. "It's a hot day. The Inspector could do with a swim."

"Thanks," Paris said. "It looks real good too. But I don't have the time now. You see, I've been assigned to do a very complicated traffic survey, and I have to report in."

"A traffic survey?" she asked. "It doesn't seem like your line of work."

"It isn't. But I'm sort of doing a penance for my sins. It

seems we had a little show at White Sands, and some of the actors didn't get onto the stage."

"I don't understand a word of it," she said. "But never mind. I want to ask you something else. Don't you ever get a vacation?"

"I get three weeks in August. How about you?"

"Well, I'll be here every weekend," she said. "And I can take my two weeks in August too. Where are you planning on going?"

"I had my eye on a place at White Sands," Paris said. "The Chief said I'd be able to rent it. I was thinking of taking that."

"Hey, that's good," Harold Dana said. "Judy's quite a swimmer. If you go by water, it's only a mile from here to White Sands. Judy can swim it easy."

"I'll do better than that." Paris grinned. "I'll swim out and meet her halfway."

www.ingramcontent.com/pod-product-compliance
Lightning Source LLC
Chambersburg PA
CBHW020649180626
46816CB00003B/1197